SUE BARTON, STUDENT NURSE

SUE BARTON
STUDENT NURSE

By

HELEN DORE BOYLSTON

Image Cascade Publishing
www.ImageCascade.com

MANUFACTURED IN THE UNITED STATES
OF AMERICA

A hardcover edition of this book was originally published by Little, Brown & Company. It is here reprinted by arrangement with the author's estate.

First *Image Cascade Publishing* edition published 2008.
Copyright renewed © 1964 by Helen Dore Boylston.

Library of Congress Cataloging in Publication Data
Dore Boylston, Helen 1895–1984.
        Sue Barton student nurse.

(Juvenile Girls)
Reprint. Originally published: New York: Little, Brown & Company.

ISBN 978-1-59511-024-4 (Pbk.)

To

ELLA P. LOCKE

The reader will understand that the institution, the staff, and the patients mentioned in this story are wholly imaginary.

CONTENTS

SUE BARTON, STUDENT NURSE

I

PROBATION BEGINS

THE train began to move at last. Sue leaned forward, her red curls crushed against the windowpane, and looked back to where her father and mother and Ted stood on the station platform. Their faces were growing smaller. Sue's resolute young mouth quivered suddenly, and her eyes misted.

Ted broke into a run and dashed down the platform, his first long trousers flapping about his legs. Opposite Sue's window and still running, he cupped his hands around his mouth.

"Mother says — " he shouted. The rest was lost.

"What?" Sue formed the word silently, with her lips.

"Mother says . . . forgot . . . rubbers . . . get some more!" Ted roared.

Sue grinned. She had not forgotten her rubbers. She had ignored them. Ted grinned back in perfect comprehension and slowed to a walk as the train gathered speed. Sue leaned back against the dusty red of the car seat and stared out of the window with unseeing eyes until the ache in her throat had subsided. The wheels, clicking over the rails beneath her, made words to which she tried not to listen.

3

"You're afraid! You're afraid! You're afraid," they said.

And she was afraid — a little — now that the moment had come. This was what the speaker at her high–school graduation had called "going out into the world." It didn't feel like that. It felt like going somewhere on a train.

Ever since Sue could remember, she had wanted to be a trained nurse. Her father, himself a doctor, had thought this an excellent idea, but everyone else had been extraordinarily discouraging about it. They spoke much and often of the hard life, though they never seemed to know exactly what made it so hard. The impression they gave was that, once the hospital doors closed behind you, you were doomed to a life of bread and water and scrubbing floors.

"I don't believe it," Sue had said obstinately to Ted. "You can't make me think that three hundred girls living together don't have any fun. And if they have to scrub floors all the time — who takes care of the patients? Elijah's ravens?"

Outside the train windows the telegraph poles snatched up tiny threads of wire which crossed and recrossed and ran together, and separated, until Sue was dizzy with watching them. It was a long time before the little towns began to be one big town, and the coach was suddenly darkened as the train slid into a great noisy station.

"All out!"

Sue gathered up her belongings and hurried out into the dark smoky station in search of a taxicab. She gave the driver the address of the hospital so grimly that he stared at her, and she wondered uncomfortably if he thought her a patient.

Once out of sight of the station the taxi moved with difficulty through swarms of dark-skinned, poorly clad children who were shouting and playing in the streets, and Sue remembered that when the hospital had been built, more than a hundred years ago, it had stood on the very outskirts of the city. But as the years passed the city crept around it until now it stood on the edge of the slums.

The taxi jolted around a corner and began to crawl down a steep hill. Sue's heart skipped a beat. There, at the foot of the hill, was the hospital. Inside high walls lay a green lawn, broad and smooth and shaded by giant elms. On three sides of the lawn buildings rose in massive irregularity against the sky, a cluster of red brick and granite. Beyond them were others, and still others. The hospital was a town in itself.

Across the back of the green rectangle of lawn was a gray building, three stories in height, but so perfectly proportioned that it seemed lower. On either side of the wide stone steps in the centre, ivied columns rose straight up into the shadow of a stately dome. The lines melted into one another in a quiet harmony of age and beauty.

"Oh!" Sue breathed.

5

The taxi driver heard her. "Yeah," he said out of the corner of his mouth. "Nice, ain't it — if you got a weakness for hospitals. I ain't. Well, here you are, miss."

The car sped through a wide gateway and stopped before a tall brick building. Sue was conscious only of its revolving door, which she pushed around too rapidly for the comfort of her heels. The letter from the hospital had said that she was to report at the Training School Office on her arrival. Where was it?

A circular booth marked "Information" faced the door. Sue approached it and was greeted by a little man who seemed to know that she was one of the new probationers, for without asking her business he said kindly: —

"The Training School Office is just back there in the rotunda — third door to your left. You can leave your bags here."

The vast, high-ceilinged rotunda was dark after the bright sunlight outside. Sue's heart was pounding as she went across it to the third door on the left. It stood open, revealing a small office with light plaster walls and dark woodwork. Four nurses in white uniforms sat at desks, writing.

They didn't look up, and Sue hesitated. After a moment she rapped. Four heads lifted, and four pairs of eyes looked at her pleasantly. Sue felt instantly shy, but in spite of it the sight of those uniforms thrilled her. These were real nurses. Sue had never seen a real nurse — except her father's office nurse, an elderly soul who

6

wore no cap, and whose uniforms were nondescript af-
fairs which did n't fit. Her own uniforms, made at home,
of blue cambric with white aprons and separate white
collars, as specified in the letter from the hospital, did n't
seem like real uniforms. They were more like house
dresses.

"I — I am Sue Barton," she ventured at last.

One of the nurses, a stout woman with white hair
and twinkling eyes, rose and came to the door.

"Oh yes, Miss Barton. How do you do? I am Miss
Mason, the assistant superintendent." She smiled at Sue
pleasantly. "Just follow me, please. And don't worry
about your bags. They will be sent over."

She rustled out into the rotunda and Sue followed her,
not knowing whether she should make conversation or
not, but liking Miss Mason's twinkling eyes.

They passed through a maze of corridors, some of
red brick with arched ceilings and rich with sunlight;
others of white plaster, chill and austere. Miss Mason's
uniform rattled in the silence until it seemed to echo.

"It's a very confusing place, is n't it?" Miss Mason said.
"But you 'll soon learn your way around."

"I hope so," Sue laughed.

She tried to fix a few landmarks in her mind, but
it was impossible. All the corridors were repetitions of
all the other corridors. The place was a great silent
labyrinth.

Occasionally, in the distance, Sue caught a glimpse
of a hurrying nurse in gray, or a young man in white.

7

There were no patients in sight, anywhere. With the exception of Miss Mason and the nurses in the office, all the nurses Sue had seen had worn gray uniforms with white bibs and aprons, and stiff collars and cuffs. Their caps were like Miss Mason's — stiff, pleated white crinoline, oval in shape and scarcely larger than a teacup. They were about three inches high in front and sloped back, each with a tiny pleated ruffle around its base. They looked very odd, Sue thought.

"The gray uniforms are worn by the student nurses," Miss Mason explained. "You'll be wearing one as soon as your three months of probation are over."

"I hope so," Sue said again. So there were three kinds of uniform. She already knew that probationers wore blue. Now it seemed that students wore gray, and graduates white. She wished Miss Mason wouldn't walk so fast. They were out of doors again, now, and going up the steps of a large brick building covered with ivy.

"This is Brewster House — the dormitory of the first- and second-year nurses and the probationers. The seniors and graduates live in Grafton Hall, which is back the way we just came. You will have some of your classes there."

Sue had a confused impression of more corridors and of many rooms, and then a languid elevator creaked them up to the fourth floor, where Miss Mason led the way down another corridor and opened the door of a small but very pleasant room, containing a bed, a bureau, a desk, and two comfortable chairs.

"This is your room, Miss Barton," Miss Mason said, smiling. "Your baggage will be sent over. Dinner for probationers is at six-thirty. Someone will come over to take you to the dining room. At eight o'clock this evening, Miss Matthews, the superintendent of nurses, will meet the new class downstairs in the living room. Until then you are free to do whatever you like."

She stepped out into the corridor and was gone.

Sue pulled off her hat and sat down on the bed, feeling as though she were marooned on a desert island composed entirely of silent rooms, silent corridors, and silent buildings.

"Hello," said a voice from the doorway. "New probationer?"

Sue turned and saw a slender, dark-haired girl in a gray uniform leaning against the door casing.

"Why, yes. I am," Sue said shyly, getting up.

"Scared?"

"Well, not exactly. Should I be?"

"Not with that red head. It ought to blaze a trail for you anywhere."

Sue's brown eyes darkened for an instant. She was still too young not to resent being teased about her hair. Then she smiled.

"Won't you come in?"

The nurse came in promptly and sat down on the bed Sue had just vacated.

"Grandma bring you over?"

"Gran — Oh! You mean Miss Mason. Yes, she did."

9

The nurse laughed. "She's a good egg. Everybody likes her."

"Aren't there any more probationers here yet?" Sue asked.

"Mercy, yes! The place is crawling with them. It's a big class this time — and that means plenty of trouble."

"But why?" Sue sat down again.

"Well, I'll tell you — new probationers are always being bright, earnest little girls, and running up to supervisors to say they understood that eating on the wards was not allowed, and has that rule been revoked on Ward So-and-So, because the nurses eat there — which makes it so nice for the nurses on that ward."

"Aren't you allowed to eat on the ward?" Sue asked. She had naturally never considered the matter.

"No, you aren't. There's a fifty-cent fine if you're caught. It's tough on the probationers, because they're always terribly hungry the first few weeks. It's the change, I suppose. And they do talk an awful lot. They talk all over the place — when they'd better keep quiet."

"What is this — propaganda for the Nurses' Protective Society?"

The nurse laughed. "Well, maybe." She rose to her feet. "Well, I've got to go back. There'll probably be umpteen w. d. and n. admissions on the ward by now, and none of the t. p. r.'s taken, and treatments to give p. r. n."

With these cryptic words she departed, leaving Sue rather dazed.

"Goodness!" she thought. "It's like another language — but it would be sort of fun to be able to speak it."

Her baggage arrived, brought by two men in blue overalls, and in the process of unpacking, the afternoon was gone before she realized it. Now and again other girls passed her door, shy girls who smiled in at her uncertainly, and Sue guessed that these were her own classmates. None of them ventured to speak to her. Some day, Sue supposed, she would know them as well as she knew her own family.

When her unpacking was finished and her room was in order, and one of the blue probationer's uniforms the hospital had requested her to have made was laid out on a chair, — just to look at, for she had not been told when she was to wear it, — Sue bathed luxuriously in a great tub in one of the bathrooms across the corridor, and got ready for dinner.

At a quarter after six no one had come for her. Perhaps she had better go downstairs and wait in the bright living room she had seen on her way in.

The living room was empty. She heard voices and footsteps and laughter everywhere, but no one came to find her. At twenty-five minutes after six she decided that there had been some mistake. After all, she could surely find her own way to the dining room. Someone would direct her.

Sue went to the door of the living room, and saw three nurses in gray hurrying down the corridor.

"Oh, please! Wait just a moment!" she called after

them. But they did not hear her. They opened a door at one side of the corridor and as they vanished through it Sue heard one of them say: —

"Run, girls! We'll be late!"

They were undoubtedly going to the dining room. Sue hesitated an instant and then ran after them.

The door through which they had gone opened on a flight of stairs which went down — somewhere. Sue could still hear the nurses' voices. She hurried down the stairs, but stopped at the foot, startled. She was in a cellar, but it was a very strange cellar.

It was brightly lighted and much too warm for comfort. On the ceiling and walls, in rigid geometric patterns, giant pipes bulged, covered with white asbestos. They creaked and groaned dismally, and Sue was positive that one of them moved an instant before she looked at it. The smell of hot paint was stifling.

She heard laughter in the distance and ran toward it, dashing out of her immediate cellar only to find herself in another exactly like it, long and narrow and white. The nurses were nowhere in sight. When she turned to go back the way she had come she was unable to find the entrance to the first cellar. Directly over her head a pipe cracked and then gave a long whistling moan.

This was not Sue's idea of a hospital, and in a sudden panic she fled wildly along under the shrieking pipes, turning into one entrance and then another. Shadows followed her and dark places yawned before her. Once, looking through the doorway, she saw a tangled heap of wooden legs piled against a wall, and she began to laugh hysterically.

At last she paused, out of breath, and leaned against a pipe, wondering if she would go on wandering here all night and all the next day, hearing voices and missing the owners of them by one turn.

"Silly!" she said aloud. "Of course there's a way out!"

She walked on soberly, came around a turn, and saw, far in the distance, a squat man in overalls dragging a huge bundle. She ran toward him, smiling in her relief. He heard her steps, looked back, and instantly his round face and drooping moustaches assumed an expression of such ferocity that Sue's smile vanished and she faltered: —

"W-would you please tell me the way out of here?"

The man roared something at her in a strange language and, dropping his bundle, approached her, brandishing a clenched fist.

Sue turned and ran — where she did not know, but anywhere to get away from that awful, fat, spidery creature. She heard his roars long after he was out of sight.

"What now?" she wondered helplessly.

She sat down on a fat pipe which was close to the floor and rested her chin in her hands. She didn't hear approaching steps and was unaware that anyone was near her until a pleasant, masculine voice said: —

"Well, well! What's all this?"

Sue sprang to her feet, prepared for the worst, and saw before her a tall, broad-shouldered young man, all in white. His short black hair was brushed straight back from his forehead, and his deep-set blue eyes were the clearest Sue had ever seen. He rested a shapely hand against the wall and looked down at her.

"Please — what time is it?" Sue demanded.

The young man looked a little startled at this unexpected question, but he glanced at his wrist watch.

"It's a quarter to seven."

"Oh!" Sue wailed. "My poor dinner! I've been chasing it for so long."

The young man threw back his head and laughed.

"Where did you come from?"

"New Hampshire — but I don't see what that has to do with it."

His laughter rang out again.

"All the way from New Hampshire to get your dinner! It hardly seems worth it. But I meant, where did you come from just now?"

"Oh!" Sue flushed. "I started from Brewster House. I made the mistake of trying to get to the dining room by myself — and I've spent practically all the best years of my life wandering around this awful place with pipes after me. Is my hair entirely white yet, or just streaked with gray?"

"Well, I wouldn't worry about it," said the young man, glancing at Sue's bright curls. "I presume you're one of the new probationers. There's a second dinner at seven. I'll take you to the nurses' dining room."

"Thank you so much. But what is this place?"

"Why, you see, every part of the hospital is connected with every other part by underground passages. The pipes are for hot water and steam heat. These subways are very convenient if you're in a hurry — there are so many short cuts."

"I'd rather take the train, if you don't mind."

He laughed again, and with a sureness which was miraculous to Sue he set out, down the long winding passages, shortening his long stride to keep pace with hers.

"I suppose it's a conventional question," he said as they moved along under the pipes, "but I'd really like to know — what do you think of the hospital?"

"I've hardly seen it yet. I've just come. And the first thing that happened was my getting lost in this ghastly basement — and then there was a man — a very fat man with a face like a seal. He — he chased me, and he roared like a seal. He didn't make a very good impression on me."

"I'm afraid you had an encounter with Tony, the Greek laundryman. He's been here a great many years. The nurses tease him, — and he really likes it, I think, — but he always pretends he's going to murder them."

"Yes, I'd noticed that. He's very realistic, isn't he?"

"He certainly is." He plunged one hand deep in a hip pocket. The laughter vanished suddenly from his eyes. "You'll have a very different impression of the hospital when you've been here awhile," he said slowly. "It's a grand old place. There's nothing like it. The medical profession is fascinating anywhere, but it's more so here — the place is so old — it has so much tradition — and it grows on you — this old hospital — until it fills your life."

"Why — I suppose it would," Sue said. "I'd never thought of it like that. I mean — I thought that learning to be a nurse would be fascinating, but I didn't know you could feel that way about a hospital itself."

"Ah, but you can — very much so."

He hesitated, and then went on in a curious far-away voice as though he were speaking to himself.

"Sometimes, when I can steal a moment in the evening, I go up into the old blue dome. It was the operating room a hundred years ago, but it's a museum now. It's seen the beginnings of some of the greatest advances in medical science."

He was silent for a moment, and then, as Sue did not speak, he continued.

"Up there one has a strange feeling of being in another world — standing in the silence, watching the moonlight travel along the blue walls, touching the ancient surgical instruments, lying in pools on the worn floor where great doctors used to stand to operate a hundred years ago. All that the hospital means is somehow concentrated in that old dome — at night — in the moonlight. I — it — gets you, you know."

They walked on together in silence. Sue was looking at the fine lines of his head, his clear-cut features, sensitive and strong. She had not known that people talked like this except in books, but he had spoken with complete naturalness.

"Thank you," she said at last. "That 's made everything quite — different."

He looked down at her with a sudden, warm smile. "Has it?" he said. "I 'm glad!"

"I suppose you 're a doctor?"

"Yes, an interne. They call us house officers here."

"How long do you have to be in the hospital?"

"A year and a half. I 've been here five months — oh, I beg your pardon — I 'm Dr. Barry — William Barry — commonly known as Bill."

"And I 'm Sue Barton."

He stopped and bowed gravely, but with twinkling eyes.

"How do you do, Miss Barton," he murmured solemnly. "How do you do — and good-bye. Your dining room is at the head of these stairs." He held out his hand. "Good luck."

Sue gave him her hand.

"Thank you," she said. "Thank you very much, Dr. Barry — for everything."

II

RULES AND MANNERS

There were other probationers at second dinner, and
Sue felt relieved. Nothing would happen to her, then,
for having missed first dinner.

The probationers' tables were along the wall at one
side of the room. There was no mistaking probationers.
They looked so chronically uncomfortable. Sue went to
one of the tables and sat down.

The vast dining room, filled with round tables seating
eight, was crowded and noisy with laughter and the
clatter of dishes. Nurses with tired eyes came and went.
They were nearly all young, and their faces, though lined
with fatigue, were alert and interested. The entire
dining room had an atmosphere of driving energy in
which the probationers were isolated bits of uncertainty.
They sat very stiffly, on the edges of their chairs, speaking
to each other with a really awful formality, and keeping
their eyes for the most part on their plates.

It was not until after dinner, when they gathered in
the living room of Brewster to meet the superintendent
of nurses, that they began to relax.

The new class was a large one. Sixty or seventy girls

gradually assembled in the living room and inspected each other with shy curiosity.

Sue had gone there direct from the dining room, and now, curled up in an armchair by the fireplace, she watched the new arrivals with eager interest.

A florid, slightly round-shouldered girl with a pretty face but untidy hair entered the room with a bound and a giggle. She began at once to talk to anyone who would listen. Her voice was loud and sharp.

"My name's Grace Holton," Sue heard her saying, and thought that Grace was hardly the right name for her.

In a corner of the room, seated at one of the writing desks, was another girl who, Sue felt instinctively, was not going to be one of her best friends. This girl was older than the others. She had poise, ease of manner, but her colorless face was so impassive as to appear hard — almost bitter.

At this moment Grace Holton, who was ranging round the room, spied Sue's red curls and pounced upon her eagerly, with a loud laugh.

"Hello! You look nice. What's your name? Can I sit by you?" She was as rollicking and clumsy as a puppy.

"Certainly," Sue returned pleasantly. "My name is Sue Barton."

"Well! You don't say!" She spoke as if Sue's name were something strange and foreign. "Say, are your folks rich?"

"Why, no." Sue was astonished and embarrassed. "Why?"

"Well, you look rich. You got sort of an air about you. Distant. And say, there's one girl in our class whose father's a millionaire. Her name's Constance Halliday. They say she comes from Chicago. What d' you suppose she's doing here? She's a little bit of a thing, not much higher'n my shoulder, and she's got on a suit that I'll bet cost a hundred dollars. I saw her when she came. A *chauffeur* brought her bags over!"

"Really?" Sue said, wondering why that should be so exciting.

"Sure! Prob'ly she's an awful snob. I hate snobs, don't you?"

Sue was uncertain what she had best reply, feeling that anything she said might be used against her.

A girl sitting on a couch at Sue's left leaned forward, interrupting Grace. Her sandy hair was so neat that it appeared to be painted on her head, and her mouth was prim.

"I beg your pardon," she said in a too well-bred voice. "I am Lois Wilmont. You are Miss Barton, I believe?" She cast a scathing look at the robust Grace.

Before Sue could reply Grace clutched at her arm.

"Oh! Looky!" she said in a piercing whisper. "That's her! That's Constance Halliday! The rich one! Isn't she a scream?"

In the great double doorway stood a small slender girl with a pale, ivory skin, thick black hair, and enormous

hazel eyes with heavy black lashes. Her air of dis-
tinction was pronounced but obviously natural. The
dark green broadcloth suit and tiny black hat looked
quite as expensive as Grace had suggested.

Grace nudged Sue violently in the ribs.

"I said, is n't she a scream?" she hissed. "Anybody 'd
think she was the Queen of Sheba. Oh, listen! Quick!
She 's saying something!"

Constance Halliday was indeed saying something, and
her innocent inquiry, dropping into the sudden silence,
was heard in every corner of the room. She had turned
to a girl who was standing near the door — a very fat
girl with curling blonde hair — and her low, clear voice
came to Sue distinctly.

"Could you tell me if there are any golf links around
here?"

Grace Holton's giggle was the only reply to this. The
fat girl only stared, wide-eyed. Constance Halliday
glanced quickly around the room at the rows of amused
eyes fixed upon her, and her face reddened.

"F'eaven's sake!" Grace said loudly to Sue. "Where
does she think she is — in a Country Club? I guess by
the time she 's put in eight hours' work a day here,
she 's not going to want to run around on any golf links.
Golf links, my eye!"

As Grace paused to draw breath a girl detached herself abruptly from a group near the fireplace, gave Grace
a scornful look, and crossed the room to Constance
Halliday with a free, swinging walk and determined

air. But she had merry brown eyes, a turned-up, freckled nose, and her hair, which was a rich brown, was coiled around her head in smooth braids.

"How do you do," she said to Constance Halliday. She spoke with deliberate clearness and Sue noticed that she had a slight English accent. "My name is Katherine Van Dyke," she went on. "I like golf, too. Perhaps we might play together sometime."

Constance Halliday gave her a grateful smile. "I'd love to," she said. "Shall we sit down somewhere?"

"Huh!" Grace remarked to Sue. "I hate people who are always snuggling up to the rich, don't you?"

"I don't know," Sue replied stiffly. "I've never known anyone who did. I think that Van Dyke girl has beautiful manners, and I think you were very rude."

Grace Holton's comment on this was never made, for at that moment a stout, dark-haired woman in a white uniform entered the room. The girls rose instinctively to their feet and stood waiting.

Miss Matthews sat down at a desk in one end of the room.

"Please be seated," she said to the assembled girls. Her voice was low and charming, the voice of a trained public speaker. Her face was very kind.

She spoke to the new probationers for nearly an hour. Her first words were the conventional ones of welcome. Then she told them of the great hospital of which they were now a part, of its tradition of service to humanity, of its high standards, of its hundred years of effort to make the profession of nursing one of the finest professions open to women. And lastly she gave them the rules governing their personal behavior. They were as follows: —

1. Nurses were not to behave in a frivolous manner on the wards or in the corridors of the hospital proper.

2. Nurses were not to go outside the hospital grounds in uniform without wearing a concealing coat, and they must remove their caps.

3. Nurses must not go to any department of the hospital unless on hospital business.

4. Nurses must not go to any ward in street clothes without permission to do so from the Training School Office.

5. Nurses were forbidden to eat on the wards.

6. They must not wear jewelry on duty.

7. Relations between nurses and house officers must be strictly professional. No student nurse would be permitted to go outside the hospital in the company of a house officer.

8. A nurse must always rise to her feet when addressed by a doctor. Student nurses must stand up in the presence of a graduate nurse, or any nurse senior to themselves in the school.

"These rules," Miss Matthews told the listening girls, "may seem unnecessarily strict at times, but there is a reason for each of them. The first duty of a nurse under any and all circumstances is to her patient. She has a grave responsibility and her manner should be in keeping with it. Personal adornment and personal pleasures must be put aside. Professional dignity and traditions must be maintained. And now — are there any questions?"

A pretty, fluffy-haired girl rose to her feet.

"Would you tell us, please, why we must always be professional with house officers?"

There was a faint ripple of laughter around the room. Miss Matthews gave the girl a shrewd look.

"The reason for that rule," she said gently, "is because the hospital authorities have found through long experience that nurses and doctors do not work together as well when the personal element is allowed to enter their relationship as when it is not."

"Thank you." The girl sat down.

Someone else rose.

"Why do we stand up, please, in the presence of a doctor?"

Miss Matthews smiled. "That seems very queer to you, does it not? But you must understand that you are rising, not to the man, but to his profession. It is a convention of the medical profession and you must obey it. It is for the same reason that you rise for a nurse who has had more experience than yourself. Are there any more questions?"

There were no more questions.

"That is all," Miss Matthews said. "You will find the rules regarding time off duty on the bulletin board. Please watch the bulletin board daily for orders or general information. Your time off duty will be arranged by Miss Cameron, your practical instructor and supervisor. Her classroom is downstairs. You will report there, in uniform, at eight-thirty to-morrow morning for inspection and your first class. Probationers attend second breakfast, at 7 A. M. Thank you — and good night."

She rose, and the class rose with her and remained standing until she had disappeared down the corridor, moving with her silent, measured tread.

When she had gone a buzz of conversation broke out.

Fragments of sentences followed Sue down the corridor.

"We 'd better get our uniforms ready to-night . . . Did you ever expect . . . My sister trained here and she said . . . If anybody thinks I 'm not going to talk to house officers they 're . . . What did *she* . . . Golf links! Imagine it! . . ."

The chatter went on as the class straggled out into the corridor. Several nurses in gray were standing around the ice-water tank near the elevator. They eyed the probationers, grinning.

"Well, youngsters, it won't be long now," one of them remarked.

"What do you mean?" Sue asked.

The nurses burst into shrieks of laughter.

"She does n't know, the poor lamb!" cried the one who had first spoken. "They don't any of them know!"

"Know what?" Sue persisted.

The rest of the probationers, flattered by any kind of attention from real nurses, crowded around to listen.

The nurse in gray assumed the manner of an undertaker addressing a bereaved family.

"To-morrow, my innocents, you will meet Miss Cameron. Pardon me — Miss Cameron will meet you." Her tones became sepulchral. "The days of your care-free youth are ended. To-morrow you will be cast into the lion's den."

"But I don't see — " Sue began.

The nurse turned to her companions.

"She doesn't see," she said gravely. They nodded solemnly.

The girl addressed Sue again. "You will see — and so soon. But I will say no more. I can't bear it. You are all so young and innocent." She wheeled with mock military precision, joined arms with her friends, and they moved away, their shoulders shaking.

The probationers stared at each other for a moment in awed silence. Grace Holton broke it.

"Gee!" she said. "I — why, I believe they were kidding us!"

"My, my! Whatever made you think that?" It was the girl with the hard face.

Grace turned on her.

"What's it to you?" she demanded hotly.

They stared at each other for a moment. Then the older girl moved away with a contemptuous smile.

"Just one big happy family, already," said a voice at Sue's elbow.

26

Sue turned. Katherine Van Dyke and Constance Halliday were standing beside her, looking after Grace, who was stalking toward the elevator. The Van Dyke girl had spoken.

"Yes, are n't we!" Sue said. "But you can't blame Grace Holton."

Katherine Van Dyke laughed.

"Those nurses were a nice cheerful lot. What do you think they meant?"

"Goodness knows. Probably they were just trying to frighten us."

"Well, they might have saved themselves the trouble. I 'm already so scared that nothing makes any difference."

It was Sue's turn to laugh.

"I guess we 're all rather scared. And I 've just managed to get myself into a mess."

"Oh, do tell us!" Constance Halliday cried.

Sue glanced over her shoulder, not wishing to make her first mistake public. The group around the tank had scattered in various directions.

"Well —" Sue began, and told them of her experience in the great basement of the hospital, but she did not tell them what Dr. Barry had said about the old blue dome. It was difficult to put into words and she felt instinctively that retelling it would make it sound ridiculous.

"How marvelous!" Constance Halliday exclaimed, when Sue had finished. "Rescued from an untimely death by a romantic young doctor. You lucky thing!"

27

"Well, lucky or not," Sue said, "I've got to go upstairs and try to put on my uniform collar so it won't fly up and hit me in the face."

"Oh, do yours do that?" Constance Halliday asked earnestly. "Mine never go near my face. I don't think they like it. They always crawl off down my back. I tried for hours this afternoon to get one to stay with me, but it would n't."

"Is it only your collars?" Katherine Van Dyke said plaintively. "You should see the way the whole uniform behaves on me. I hitch it here and I hitch it there, but it eludes me. My apron sort of faints away in the back and looks like a court train. My collar is n't content with slapping me in the face — it tries to decapitate me."

They looked at each other with mutual appreciation.

"See here," Sue offered. "Why don't you two bring your uniforms to my room and try them on? Maybe between us we can get them right."

"I'd love to!"

"Righto!"

They went gayly up the three flights of stairs, scorning the elevator. Brewster House had suddenly become a very pleasant place.

In the process of struggling with collars and aprons they became Kit and Sue and Connie to each other. When the refractory collars had been firmly pinned in place, and the girls were dressed again in their everyday clothes, they settled back to talk.

"How did you happen to come here?" Sue asked Kit.

28

"I don't know exactly," Kit said, stretching herself out on Sue's bed. "I've always been in difficulties at home. I'm the third of five children, you know. Father and Mother sent me to a convent school, — after the night I slid down the waterspout outside my bedroom to go to a dance, — hoping to make a little lady of me, you see. I hated the convent, so I ran away. There was a young doctor — a friend of my brothers. He was always talking about this hospital — and before I knew it, here I was."

Connie had been listening to this recital with a wistful look in her hazel eyes.

"How thrilling!" she said enviously. "You girls seem to have had a lot of fun." She was sitting sedately in the only rocking-chair.

"Have n't you had any fun?" Kit demanded.

"Not very much. I had so many governesses — and I was n't allowed to play with other children. I went to school in Paris for a while, but it was a dreary place."

"How awful!" Kit said, thinking of her own rollicking childhood. "But what are you doing here, of all places?"

"Well, you see — " Connie hesitated, and then went on — "my mother does n't like me very much, and when I came out, in Chicago, and would n't marry any of the men she picked out for me, she did n't much care what I did. But Daddy — darling Daddy — suggested that I might like to take up some kind of work. I'd been reading a lot about nursing — and it seemed such a marvelous profession — and this hospital is so famous — so — so I came."

"Whew!" Kit and Sue stared at her. Her life seemed much more exciting than theirs, but not to be liked by one's mother was beyond their comprehension.

"And now — what about you, Sue?" Connie asked.

But at that instant a bell began to ring, long and loudly. A moment later a nurse in gray stopped before the open door of Sue's room. The three girls scrambled to their feet.

"It's ten o'clock, youngsters," the nurse said kindly. "That bell means lights out. You should have been in your rooms before this. Now you'll have to undress in the dark. I'm the Student Government proctor," she explained, smiling. "Scamper, now, or I shall have to report you."

Kit and Connie gathered up their uniforms, said goodnight to Sue, and vanished down the corridor.

Sue undressed slowly in the darkness, and paused before she got into bed to look out of the window. Last night at this time she had been looking out of the window of her little room at home, hearing the sound of the sea, watching the slow stars move about it.

Now the long-dreamed-of hospital lay before her, its massive rectangles black against the sky. Around it the city purred softly, and from somewhere far away Sue heard the sudden thin clamor of an ambulance gong.

"I'm going to love this," she thought.

III

THE SALT OF THE EARTH

THE shattering scream of a rising bell woke Sue at six o'clock. She lay quiet, listening to the thud of feet over her head and in the corridors. Doors banged. Water roared in the bathrooms. There was scurrying, laughter, and the murmur of sleepy voices.

The early morning air was sharp with cold and, judging by the sound, some of the nurses were dressing in the corridor around the radiator. Probationers' breakfast was not until seven, but there was that difficult blue uniform — perhaps she had better get up now.

Sue got out of bed gingerly, for the floor was cold, closed her windows, and turned on the heat. The instant response of the radiator was consoling. Sue's fingers shook with excitement as she dressed. She was very wide-awake now.

A knock at her door startled her.

"Come in!" she called.

The door swung open and Kit and Connie stood before her in blue and white. The three girls surveyed each other's uniforms for a moment in silence. Then they began to laugh.

"Dear me!" Connie murmured and, stepping forward,

shook hands with Sue. "Nurse Barton, I presume?" she said.

Sue bowed. "No, madame, you have made a mistake. I'm the iceman."

Kit interrupted them.

"Were you thinking of having breakfast, or don't you care for food?"

The nurses in the dining room, evidently night nurses, watched the probationers with amusement. Rumors flew about concerning Miss Cameron and her classes, and the tension at the probationers' table increased. Miss Cameron was said to be utterly terrifying. Her word about any probationer was taken by the Training School Office as absolute.

"They say," Grace Holton announced breathlessly, "that if you make a single mistake you'll be sent home!"

"That's silly," someone else interposed.

"Well, I don't care. Anyway, they do say that whether you are accepted or not at the end of your probation depends on what she thinks of you."

"Then I'm finished now," Kit said. "Teachers always suspect me of the worst the moment they lay eyes on me."

"Really," Lois Wilmont said stiffly, "I'm surprised at you, Miss Van Dyke. If you do your work I can't see any reason why you should have trouble with your teachers."

Kit gazed at her solemnly. "No," she said, with her crisp English accent, "I'm sure you wouldn't, Miss Wilmont. There's something about you — "

Lois unbent. "Do you think so? That's very nice of

32

you, I'm sure. I haven't the slightest fear of Miss Cameron. I expect we shall get on perfectly. If you'll just come to me for advice — "

Sue's eye encountered Kit's and she choked. She stood up, pushing back her chair. "I think we'd better be going, girls," she said.

Her two friends followed her from the dining room, and by the time they had reached the big main corridor their laughter had subsided.

"That girl can't be real," Connie said. "Nobody is as obvious as that, or as stilted."

"She's real, all right," Kit said.

"But she sounds like a character in a badly written book. You know — one of these people who should be labeled 'Virtue' from the very first page. I've never seen anyone so self-righteous in my life."

"You were marvelous, Kit," Sue said. "How on earth do you do it? She should have been squashed flat."

Kit grinned. "It's an old English custom. I was born in Canada, you know, but my parents are both English. Anyway, it was all wasted this time. It went right over her head."

As they went up the steps to Brewster House the dark hints of the nurses came back to Sue, strengthened by the rumors at the breakfast table. Kit, suddenly subdued, pushed open the door, and in silence the three went to the stairs which led to Miss Cameron's classroom.

At the foot of the stairs the girls found themselves in a brick basement and face to face with a sink. At its left were two doors, one opening on a laboratory, the other on a tiny linen closet. On the right was another door through which they could see rows of straight-backed chairs, each with one wide arm, and all facing an invisible part of the room.

"Of course, we *would* have to be the first here," Connie whispered.

Sue said nothing. It was absurd that her heart should be beating so fast. Drat those nurses and their hints!

In single file the girls entered the classroom.

There was no one there. The chairs faced a low platform on which were a single small table, a chair, and a bed. Across one side of the room, against the wall, were perhaps ten more beds. It was the bed on the platform, however, which held the girls' attention, for in it, limp and ridiculous, lay a gigantic rubber doll, the bedclothes tucked up to its chin. Its painted eyes, very definitely crossed, stared up at the ceiling.

For a moment the girls confronted it in amazement. Then Kit giggled, and all three burst into shrieks of laughter which they instantly stifled.

"Ah," said Connie, in her quick, low voice, "it must be Miss Cameron, resting before class."

"Unfortunate about her eyes, is n't it?" Sue said in tones of sympathy.

"You 'd better be careful," Kit said. "Maybe it 's sensitive. I say, it is spooky, is n't it?"

There was a sound of steps on the stairs and the girls sat down hastily in the front row of chairs.

"This is a mistake," Kit said under her breath to Sue.
"The front row is no place for me."

"Shh-sh-sh!"

They turned toward the door and saw entering it —
Lois Wilmont.

"Enter Napoleon," Kit murmured.

Behind Lois came the rest of the class, talking and
laughing. Lois walked over to the doll in the bed and
inspected it gravely. Then she nodded approval.

"Not Napoleon — Cæsar's wife!" Sue whispered.

"Everything all right, Miss Wilmont?" Kit called.

"Very interesting," Lois returned without looking up.
"But it really ought — "

"Hey, Willie! You'd better get away from that!"
Grace Holton giggled.

The class, settling itself in the chairs, grinned in delight.
Poor Lois was labeled as "Willie" from that moment.

The very fat and pretty girl to whom Connie had addressed her remark about the golf links appeared suddenly
in the doorway. She was out of breath and her eyes were
enormous.

"Oh, my gosh! She's coming, girls!"

Her tone was more alarming than any description could
have been.

There was an instant silence. Not an apron rustled.
The class sat rigid, all eyes on the door.

Something white loomed outside and bore down on the
class with a rhythmic, bounding walk. Sue caught her
breath, conscious only of a pair of keen blue eyes sweep-

ing over the class, and a wide, stern mouth, clamped shut. Miss Cameron strode across the room to the platform, mounted it, and paused beside the table. The iron mouth relaxed in a smile.

"Good morning, young women." Her voice had a slight grating quality.

The class murmured something, staring, dazed, at the compact powerful figure and small head. Miss Cameron was in white from head to foot. Even on her cap she wore no black velvet band — the black band of the graduate nurse. Miss Mason had worn one, and so had Miss Matthews.

Miss Cameron called the roll, and Sue, watching, knew that every name and every face would be remembered.

When the last girl on the list had answered to her name, Miss Cameron looked at the class in silence, and in that moment, so briefly that it was as though a veil had been withdrawn and instantly replaced, her features softened. The impenetrability vanished from her eyes and they were kind. She looked at the class as one looks at an unsuspecting puppy which *must* be housebroken. The room was warm and very still. To the probationers sitting there, it had become the universe.

Miss Cameron's face resumed its sternness as she spoke.

"After to-day you will be grouped in three sections. Your name and the number of your section will appear on the bulletin board, with the hours of your classes and your time off duty. Rise, please!"

The class scrambled to its feet, startled.

"Please line up at the back of the room!"

In a confusion of scraping chairs and dropping pens the class lined up, expectant. Miss Cameron descended from the platform and walked slowly along the line, her face becoming more grim with every step.

"If that's the way you put on your clothes at home, I'm surprised that your family allowed you to go out of the house."

The girl addressed looked down at her uniform in bewilderment.

"Your apron is twisted and your collar is under one ear!"

She turned as if to go, and then came back with a pounce. "Your stockings! Wrinkled! And what kind of heels are those for a nurse? High heels! Get yourself some proper shoes this afternoon!"

She moved on, to stop again before Lois Wilmont with a look of horror. Her eyes were riveted on Lois's hands. The smug expression faded slowly from Lois's face. Her high color receded, leaving her white and strained.

"Take off that jewelry!"

"That jewelry" was a tiny signet ring on Lois's little finger. Lois tugged at it, fumbling in her nervousness.

"A nurse never wears jewelry on duty. It's unsanitary."

She went on down the line.

"Miss Van Dyke!"

"Yes, Mi—"

"Yes! Yes, what? Have you no manners? What

37

kind of home have you come from? Yes, *Miss Cameron!*"

"Ye-yes, *Miss Cameron.*"

"Your aprons are too long! Have them shortened in the sewing rooms!"

"Yes, Miss Cameron."

"*Miss Holton!*"

Grace jumped as though stung and giggled hysterically.

"What are you gaping at? Take that stupid grin off your face. And stand up straight. Your hair is untidy. This is not a football field."

"No-no, Miss Cameron. I — I mean, yes, Miss Cameron."

"Say what you mean! Don't talk nonsense."

Sue was next, holding her breath. Miss Cameron looked at her quite awfully, and Sue felt as though a cold wind were blowing upon her.

"Pull your belt down."

Sue pulled it down, and Miss Cameron passed on. Sue breathed again.

"Miss Halliday, your collar is crawling down your back. The young people of to-day are always in such haste. Take the proper amount of time and fasten it as it should be."

"Yes, Miss Cameron."

Sue's lips twitched, remembering how Connie had struggled with that collar.

Down the line the white figure went, leaving consternation behind it. At the end Miss Cameron turned and faced the class.

38

"I don't know what the hospital is coming to, I'm sure. You all ought to be at home with your mothers. This is no place for irresponsible, scatterbrained young women. You don't look as if you would be able to find your way around alone. I only hope you will make good nurses, and not have to be dismissed. Come with me, now, and keep your attention on what I am saying."

She crossed the room with her bounding stride and opened a closet door. The class crowded behind her with alacrity. The closet contained a miscellaneous collection of objects — string, scissors, glue, and bandages predominating.

"You will memorize all the equipment of the classroom and know the exact place for everything. The classroom has the same equipment as the wards, arranged in the same way. If you know where to find things here, you will be able to find those same things instantly on any ward." She added in an ominously lowered voice, "I don't want to find balls of twine in the sink, or rubber sheets in the medicine closet."

She closed the door, surged around a corner, and was gone. The probationers exchanged uncertain glances and then followed her. They were introduced to the linen closet, with its blankets, pillow slips, and sheets, snowy white against the dark walls, all in precise V-shaped piles; then the laboratory glowing with the reds, blues, greens, and yellows of antiseptics in great five-pint bottles. In the golden-bronze of copper racks poultice pans gleamed. Crimson boxes of rubber tubing and rubber gloves lay along the lower shelves. A row of surgical instruments glittered from a glass case.

"Oh!" Sue whispered, unconscious that she had spoken.

"Well! What is it, Miss Barton?"

"I — the colors are so lovely, Miss Cameron."

Miss Cameron looked at her sharply and at that moment someone tittered. Miss Cameron whirled on the offender.

"What's funny about that? Miss Barton is right. It is beautiful. I'm glad she has the imagination to see it." She turned to Sue again. "You seem an intelligent young woman, Miss Barton, but I hope you are not going to spend all your time in daydreaming."

"No, Miss Cameron."

But Miss Cameron was already on her way back to the classroom, where she stepped up on the platform and turned to look at the wavering class.

"Come! Come! What's all this straggling? What are you waiting for? Do you have to be told everything to do — like a lot of trained monkeys? Take your seats at once!"

The probationers scurried to their chairs.

There followed clear and concise instructions on the proper way to clean a refrigerator, to sweep, and to dust.

"There will be no time this morning," Miss Cameron said in conclusion, "for your first lesson in bed making. That will be taken up to-morrow. You will be provided with notebooks. On the bulletin board you will find the list of wards to which you are assigned for duty. You will proceed now to Grafton Hall for your class in anatomy, and after that go to your wards. That is all. Class dismissed."

The probationers almost fled from the room. Upstairs in the hallway they seethed before the bulletin board, talking in short, breathless sentences.

"I'll never be able to stand that every day — gosh, I've never been so scared in my life. . . . Me, too, I'm a wreck! . . . What *do* you suppose she'll do to us to-morrow? . . . Oh, look, every one of us is off duty at four-thirty. . . . Where, for goodness' sake, is Ward I? . . . Who's the girl who thinks pots and pans are beautiful — did you ever hear . . ."

Sue felt a hand on either arm. Kit and Connie were beside her, and the three stood together, presenting a solid front to the world at large.

"Where are we on duty?" Kit asked.

"I don't know — let's see — we're in the same section, anyway."

The wards listed beside their names meant nothing to them. Sue, looking down the list, saw that she was assigned to Ward 23. So was someone named Hilda Grayson. That would be the fat girl, Sue thought, and turned to look for her, but she was gone, and the group around the bulletin board was thinning rapidly.

"What do you suppose it will be like on the wards?" Connie said. "I'm excited, are n't you?"

"Well, how did your practical-nursing class go?"

The three friends turned, to see, standing close behind them, a nurse in gray, wearing a black band on her cap. This seemed unusual. Judging by her gray uniform, she was a student. Graduates wore black bands — and this band was only about half as wide as those of the graduates.

The nurse was smiling — not with the familiar, jeering amusement, but with sympathy. She looked, Sue thought, as if she had just stepped out of a stained-glass window or off a Greek coin. She was too lovely to be real, and she had a natural dignity which was very impressive.

Kit was the first to speak.

"It was ghastly," she said.

"What — what makes her so violent?" Connie asked.

Sue, the practical, said thoughtfully, "Is she really like that inside, or is it the policy of the hospital to scare probationers into fits, to see who can stand it?"

The nurse laughed. "You poor lambs," she said. "Well, we've all been through it." She turned to Sue. "My dear child, don't get that idea into your head. The hospital has nothing to do with Miss Cameron's methods. She belongs to the old type of nursing instructor who doesn't believe in sparing the rod and spoiling the child."

"Oh, dear!" Sue wailed.

"Not at all. She's the salt of the earth."

"I never did like salt," Kit said.

The nurse laughed.

"Don't feel that way. You'll have a hard time in her classes, but you'll find that she's absolutely fair. She's a splendid teacher — you won't forget anything you learn in her class. And her standard of nursing is something to take off your hat to. This hospital has been taking off its hat to her for twenty-five years."

"But weren't you afraid of her?"

"Of course. I still am. Everybody is. She's unique."

"She certainly is," said the irrepressible Kit.

"Well, you'll feel differently about her when you've finished with her classes."

"Would you tell us, please," said Sue, "what is that black band you are wearing?"

The nurse flushed. "Oh, that's the student head nurse's band."

"Are you a *head nurse?*" The girls were impressed.

"Why not? You have to know how to run a ward before you graduate — and I'm nearly through. You'll have one some day." She paused, and then added, "There's another black band which you will see around — the senior band. It's called the 'shoestring' because it's so narrow. It doesn't mean that the nurse wearing it is a senior in the school, necessarily. It simply means that she has been longest on a certain ward, and is in charge when the head nurse is off duty."

"Thank you!" the girls chorused.

"Not at all. I'll be glad to tell you anything you want to know at any time. I was a probationer once myself.

And now — you'd better run along or you'll be late to theory."

"Oh, goodness! Thank you — again."

They hurried away down the long corridor feeling that they had been initiated into mysteries.

IV

"NIZE-A GIRL"

THE theory class was quite like any class in high school, except that the instructor wore a uniform and cap. She passed around notebooks, textbooks on anatomy and physiology, and a book on medicines and their action, called "Therapeutics."

During the first part of the lecture the class was disconcerted by the presence of a large skeleton in one corner of the classroom, but before the period was over they had almost forgotten it.

Their first out-of-class assignment was a request to learn, before to-morrow, the name and location of every bone in the human body. This would not be difficult, the instructor assured them comfortably, as there were only two hundred bones exclusive of the teeth.

The class gasped.

As the hour drew to an end Sue began to think about the ward with growing excitement. After all, it was being on a real ward, with real patients, which would be the great experience. Sue wondered if she would have to see anything very dreadful. That was the one idea people seemed to have about a hospital, and about being a nurse.

"You'll see such awful things," they always said.

Sue hoped she would n't faint, or anything. And she did so hope the patients would like her. They were just people, she reassured herself. She would be charming and gentle and very sympathetic, and they would be comforted just in seeing her about. It was a pleasant thought.

But on the way to the ward she had a few misgivings. Fat Hilda Grayson toiled up the stairs to Ward 23 beside her, panting that she had heard that all head nurses were devils who jumped down your throat for nothing at all and reported you to the Training School Office without any reason.

"I 'm scared," Hilda said frankly.

"Nonsense!" Sue's confidence was returning as Hilda's nervousness increased. "It has n't been very awful so far, has it?"

Hilda paused to lean against the iron balustrade.

"Wait — a — minute," she begged. "You go — up — these stairs like — a steam engine. What d' you mean — not — very — awful? I suppose you 'd call Miss Cameron's — class just — a rest hour."

Sue laughed.

"No, I would n't. But we had plenty of warning about her. Nobody 's warned us about the wards, so there can't be anything to worry about."

"I 've been warned," said Hilda gloomily. Her breath was coming more easily now. "I 've just been telling you."

They went on up the winding stone stairs. At the second landing a sign pointing to the left read, "Ward 23."

They turned the corner, passed a vast dim linen closet, and found themselves in the door of the ward.

Sue caught her breath and Hilda gave a faint moan.

There were patients everywhere — women in red woolen bathrobes who walked stiffly, women sitting heavy and inert on chairs, women who were just faces on pillows. White beds stood against the walls all around the room, and the sunlight slanted across them, lying in golden squares on the brown floor, gleaming dully on chair arms and table tops. The ward was hushed in spite of a low murmur of voices. There was a strong smell of soapsuds.

Two nurses were making beds at one end of the ward. A third nurse was sitting at a desk in the centre of the ward, and Sue realized with a slight shock that the face of this nurse was familiar. There was no mistaking the clear purity of that profile, or the cleft chin. It was the student head nurse who had talked to them that morning by the bulletin board.

Everything would be all right now.

Sue hurried across to the desk, followed by the still reluctant Hilda.

"Good morning. We've come to report for duty."

The head nurse looked up.

"Good morning," she said cordially. Then she recognized Sue and smiled, not with her mouth but with her eyes. They were clear gray eyes with heavy black lashes. "Well! So you are going to be one of my probationers. Which of you is which?"

47

"I'm Hilda Grayson," said Hilda eagerly, and Sue thought that Hilda's ideas about head nurses seemed to be undergoing a rapid change.

"I'm Sue Barton."

"Thank you. And I am Miss Waring. Let's see — I've got your time off duty on my slip here — you're both off duty at four-thirty. Mercy! I've got to find things for you to do until then, and you aren't allowed to do anything until you've been taught how to do it by Miss Cameron." She raised an eyebrow at the two girls, who smiled back, completely charmed.

Miss Waring rose.

"Come and meet the other nurses."

In the kitchen they were introduced to a small, dark girl who was putting knives and forks and spoons on brass trays and stacking the trays in a pile. Her name was Miss Harris. She spoke to the girls pleasantly and continued to stack trays. They returned to the ward where the two nurses were making beds. One of them, a heavily built girl with sandy hair and a freckled face, wore the "shoe-string" band around her cap, and Sue knew that she was the ward senior. This was Miss White. The other nurse, Miss Folsom, still wore the probationer's blue, but she had her cap. Both girls nodded affably to Sue and Hilda and went on with their work.

"Miss Grayson," Miss Waring said in her quiet voice, "you had better help Miss Harris with the dish work. She will tell you what to do."

Hilda hurried away, anxious to please.

48

"Now, Miss Barton, I'm going to send you to X-ray with a patient. It's all right," she added, as Sue looked alarmed. "You don't have to do anything. The orderly will wheel her down. Just go with her, and wait outside until the X-ray people are through with her."

When Sue returned from a completely uneventful trip to X-ray with a very bored and sleepy patient who didn't appear to need comforting, she found that the patients' lunches had arrived. They came up on a dumb-waiter and the food was put into a steam table and served from there.

The tiny kitchen was very hot. All the nurses were there, including Hilda, and all stepping on each other's feet. Trays clashed. The steam table hissed. Dishes clattered. Inside, the ward buzzed in expectation.

"You can help with the trays," Miss Waring told Sue. "The special diets have been served. There are only the regular house diets left. You can't get into trouble with those. Just bring in the trays as fast as they are ready and give them to the patients who haven't any."

This was Sue's opportunity. Now she could talk to the patients and make them feel that she was sympathetic and to be depended upon. So far there had certainly been no awful sights. The patients were either up and around, or lying quietly in bed. Nobody seemed to be miserable. Sue felt quite light-hearted and confident. This was going to be fun.

She took in the first tray, set it down on the bedside table, and opened her mouth to speak. The patient, a stout woman with iron-gray hair and a red face, looked at her sourly.

"Pretty young, ain't you?"

"I — why, yes."

"Sixteen? Seventeen?"

"I'm eighteen," Sue said with dignity.

"Well, you don't look it."

Sue retired to the kitchen, vanquished.

The next patient was a mousy little woman who smiled at Sue consolingly.

"My, you poor child! You're dretful young to be in a hospital."

Sue tried to smile.

Miss White came in with a tray, set it down by the patient in the next bed, and stood looking down at the woman, her blue eyes twinkling. She looked very big and solid and tolerant. When she spoke her voice had a heartiness which brought a responsive smile to the patient's face.

"Come on, now, Mrs. McCarthy. No bluffing this time. Puddings are to eat — not to dump into ice-water pitchers."

The patient grinned in delight.

"Shure an' I never thought ye seen that, Miss White."

"You'd be surprised," Miss White said with meaning, and the patient looked both pleased and guilty.

"Ain't she the grand gurl," Mrs. McCarthy said to Sue's patient when Miss White had gone.

Sue felt very inadequate. She could never in this world be hearty like that.

She felt somewhat cheered later, however, when she found that the shy and quiet Miss Folsom got on just as well with the patients as did Miss White.

"This isn't as easy as I'd expected," Sue thought. "I guess I'll just have to work out a way of my own with them."

When lunch was over and all the trays had been collected, Sue and Hilda were sent to their own lunch. On their return Sue was greeted by Miss White in the door of the ward.

"I've got a job for you, Miss Barton." She indicated a patient who was wandering about the ward — a large Italian woman who wore a perpetual scowl. One arm was in a sling. Sue wondered what was the matter with her, but was too shy to ask.

"It's Mrs. Pasquale, there," Miss White went on. "She can't seem to talk without using her hair as an exclamation point. I've combed it once — and now look at it. See if you can't make her look a little less like a Zulu gone mad, before visiting hour."

Sue hurried to the laboratory for a comb and towel and, returning, approached Mrs. Pasquale, trying to look firm and efficient.

"Miss White wants me to comb your hair, Mrs. Pasquale," she said gently.

The woman stared at her, uncomprehending.

"She don't speak English, miss," one of the patients explained.

"Thank you," said Sue. She pointed to the comb and to Mrs. Pasquale's hair. "Come," she said.

"No come!" said Mrs. Pasquale with violence.

Sue stood, helpless and mortified, wondering what she had best do, when a voice spoke behind her — Miss White's.

"Here! Here! What's all this? No nonsense now, Mrs. Pasquale." She propelled the woman to a chair, laughing and talking to her, and to Sue's surprise Mrs. Pasquale sat down meekly.

"She won't listen to anybody but Miss White and Miss Waring," one of the patients told Sue. "I guess you got a job on your hands."

Mrs. Pasquale's hair was in two braids, tied together at the ends with a single worn piece of narrow red ribbon. Sue removed it and laid it carefully on the table behind her. She unbraided the curling black hair and began to comb it as gently as she could, but her hands shook with nervousness and she was very conscious of Mrs. Pasquale's sullen face.

One side had been combed and rebraided and Sue was beginning on the other when Mrs. Pasquale muttered something suddenly. Sue started, and her comb struck a snarl at the same moment. Mrs. Pasquale heaved herself to her feet with a yell of rage which brought Miss White and Miss Waring to the spot instantly.

"Never mind," Miss Waring said to Sue. "White,

you'd better finish her hair." She laid a hand on Sue's shoulder. "Run out and see if you can do anything in the kitchen."

Sue went, deeply mortified. Why did she have to make a mess of the very first thing she did? Now Miss Waring would think she wasn't any good. But still, it was a relief to escape from that violent Italian voice. There was no one in the kitchen. She tried the laboratory, and found Miss Folsom boiling rubber gloves in a little copper sterilizer.

"I'll watch those for you," Sue said eagerly.

Miss Folsom thanked her and disappeared.

It was scarcely a minute later that Sue heard a commotion in the ward — a commotion which came nearer and nearer. There were shrieks which could have been made by no one but Mrs. Pasquale. Miss White's voice and Miss Waring's blended in expostulation.

The shrieks reached the doorway, where Mrs. Pasquale caught sight of Sue.

She uttered a yell which outdid any of her previous attempts in volume, broke loose from restraining hands, and lumbered forward. Her black eyes, fixed on Sue's face, glittered with malice. Her features were purple with emotion. The just-combed hair stood out in all directions. Miss White and Miss Waring, following behind her, were helpless with laughter.

Sue backed against the wall and tried to look amused.

Mrs. Pasquale bore down upon her, shrieking, thrust her hand roughly into Sue's blouse pocket, withdrew it, and pawed at her apron. Her breath was hot on Sue's neck.

"Wha — what's the matter with her?" Sue gasped.

"I have n't the least idea." Miss Waring had seized the groping hand and was holding it firmly. "White, go over to 27 and get that little Italian nurse to come here."

In the middle distance Sue caught a glimpse of Hilda, staring horrified, and beyond her Miss Folsom and Miss Harris.

The Italian nurse was tiny and plump and capable. She hurled one staccato question into the tumult and Mrs. Pasquale turned to her, raging. The dishes rattled with the vibration of that voice. Mrs. Pasquale stamped. She tore at her hair. She shook her fist in Sue's face. She wailed. She screamed.

At last the Italian nurse remarked placidly, "She says this probationer stole her red hair ribbon."

"Oh, mercy!" Miss Waring exclaimed, and even Sue managed a smile at this.

Mrs. Pasquale, looking from face to face, suddenly broke out again, and was silenced by a single word from her interpreter.

Sue found her voice. "But I did n't," she said.

"Don't be absurd, child. Of course you did n't," Miss Waring laughed.

Mrs. Pasquale raged anew, and wept.

"Tell her," Miss Waring said, "that we 'll get her another."

This was explained to Mrs. Pasquale, who replied violently.

"She says she wants that one." The Italian nurse was apologetic. "She says if she catches this girl alone she'll take that ribbon away from her and she'd better look out."

"And you tell her," said Miss Waring, "that if she does n't behave herself I'll call Dr. Barry."

Sue heard the name with a slight shock, and so, apparently, did Mrs. Pasquale, for she wilted.

"No," she said in a quieter voice. "No Dr. Barry."

"*Allora!*" The Italian nurse made a gesture of finality and the little scene was over.

At least it appeared to be over, for Mrs. Pasquale went back into the ward. But Sue was uncomfortably aware that those black eyes followed her whenever she was in sight. During visiting hour Mrs. Pasquale's daughter came in, and they both watched Sue.

"Shure an' she's loony," Mrs. McCarthy told Sue. "Don't ye mind her, dearie. Them foreigners is always a queer lot."

Hilda looked at Sue as one looks at a person doomed.

"Gee, Barton!" she said. "I would n't be you for anything."

"My, you *are* a comfort!" Sue retorted. "She'll probably choke me in some dark corner — and then *you'll* have to comb her hair to-morrow."

"Don't!" Hilda shuddered.

Miss Waring was more reassuring. "Don't let this

55

worry you," she said. "She'll have forgotten all about it by to-morrow."

"I hope so." Sue felt a little better. At least no one believed that she had taken the ribbon. But there were still those eyes, following her every move. They bored into her back when she collected the visitors' permits. They scorched her when she hurried into the ward with drinks for the patients. Later, when the clean laundry came, and Sue went into the linen closet to help Miss White put it away, a shadow lurked outside the door and a low muttering went on.

"For goodness' sake! That old devil is still after you," Miss White said with a chuckle. "Look out she does n't take a sock at you. It would be like her."

Sue's chin came up at that, but she said nothing.

The afternoon dragged on, with Mrs. Pasquale staring from doorways, appearing out of nowhere to scowl horribly, wandering after Sue as she hurried in and out of the ward. And Sue wished, as she had never wished anything before, that she were safely at home and had never heard of the hospital.

Four-thirty came at last. Sue went in to Miss Waring to report off duty and found Hilda arranging the belongings of a patient in a table drawer.

"Don't wait for me," Hilda said. "I'm not quite through."

Sue went on to Miss Waring, who looked up with a smile.

"Good night, Miss Barton. I'm sorry you've had such a miserable time your very first day on duty."

"It doesn't matter," Sue assured her. "Good night — and thank you."

As Sue passed Hilda on her way out that young lady hissed dramatically, "Look out! She's coming after you!"

Sue glanced back. Mrs. Pasquale's table drawer was open. She had turned from it and was coming down the ward, but to Sue's relief she went on by.

"Crape hanger!" Sue said to Hilda, and hurried out. But at the door of the ward she stopped short.

A dark figure with glittering eyes stood in the shadow by the linen-closet door.

It was too much. "If I have to face that woman again," Sue thought, "I'll start talking Italian myself." She looked around her in desperation. If she could just hide somewhere until Mrs. Pasquale grew tired of waiting, and then slip past the linen closet and down the stairs — Ah! There was a place!

In the passageway to the laboratory was a small door, evidently a closet of some kind, probably a broom closet. It was out of sight of that lurking shadow. Sue went over to it casually, jerked open the door, and stepped in, looking over her shoulder as she did so, to make certain that Mrs. Pasquale had not seen her.

She stepped in and dropped — through bottomless space.

57

Warm darkness and rushing air engulfed her. Down and down she fell, too shocked to think or feel, conscious only of smooth walls shooting past her. Then she struck bottom — soft and yielding bottom which received her gently.

For a moment Sue lay still, dazed but unhurt. Then she sat up. It was too dark to see anything, but she felt about, encountering masses of crumpled cloth, the softness of wool. She looked up. Far above her, so far that the light from the door through which she had fallen was only a tiny spot on a smooth round shaft, something moved. Then a sepulchral voice boomed down the shaft.

"Mamma mia!"

It was Mrs. Pasquale! Her head came into the shaft, almost blotting out the light. Well, she could n't get at Sue here, certainly. Sue smiled in shaky triumph.

She knew now where she was. She had fallen down a laundry chute. A sudden, dreadful thought occurred to Sue as Mrs. Pasquale's head vanished. What if she did n't tell anyone what had happened? Sue would not be missed. Everyone supposed that she had gone off duty. It would be impossible to make herself heard, even if she yelled at the top of her voice, and surely no soiled laundry would be collected before morning!

She scrambled to her feet in a sudden panic. What if somebody dumped a lot of laundry down? She'd be smothered! Her heart was pounding wildly as she felt around the smooth walls of her prison. There was nothing — no — yes — there *was* a door, — she could feel the cracks under her fingers, — but it was fastened from the outside.

Sue drew in a deep breath and was about to scream when another voice came down the shaft — Miss Waring's.

"Miss Barton! Miss Barton!"

"*Yes!*" Sue roared, and was astounded at the power of her lungs.

"Are you hurt?"

"No, not at all. But I think I 'm having a nervous breakdown!"

"So is everybody else! Miss Folsom has gone to the basement to let you out. We 'll have you free in just a minute."

Mrs. Pasquale had gone for help after all.

There were steps outside. Hands fumbled with the door of the chute. It opened and Sue stepped out into the welcoming arms of Miss Folsom, who clutched her thankfully.

"Are you all right?"

"Yes, of course."

"Thank goodness there was laundry in the shaft, or you 'd — " she broke off with a shudder.

"Be bouncing yet," Sue finished for her. "Well, there was laundry, so let 's not think about it. I 'm fearfully sorry to have made such a fool of myself." She explained how she happened to fall.

"Mrs. Pasquale nearly had a fit," Miss Folsom said.

"She all but tore off Miss Waring's uniform trying to get her to understand. We had to get Miss Olivetti over from 27 again. We — we all thought you had been killed."

They had reached the basement stairs and Miss Folsom added, "You'll have to come back to the ward and let everybody see that you're alive. Besides, Mrs. Pasquale insists on seeing you."

Sue groaned.

The entire ward seemed to be waiting at the head of the stairs outside 23.

"Are you sure you're all right?" Miss Waring greeted her.

"Yes — really. I don't think I'm doomed to fall into an early grave — I'm just going to be scared into one."

Miss Waring laughed, but she was very pale.

Mrs. Pasquale appeared suddenly, towing Miss Olivetti, and pushed her way roughly through the crowd of patients and nurses around Sue. The patients backed away as from a firecracker.

Sue braced herself.

The shrieking staccato Italian began again and Sue thought dully that whoever said Italian was a beautiful language ought to meet Mrs. Pasquale.

"She says," Miss Olivetti translated, "that she's very sorry she made you so much trouble. She says she has found her ribbon. It was in her drawer. She was coming to tell you, but you ran away and jumped down a black hole."

"But why did n't she tell me in the ward instead of being ghostly in the linen closet?"

Miss Olivetti spoke rapidly to Mrs. Pasquale, who hung her head like a naughty child and replied in a low voice.

"She says she was ashamed and did n't want to say she was sorry in front of the ward. She was afraid they'd laugh at her."

"Don't any of you dare laugh," Miss Waring said. The patients melted away, smothering their grins.

Mrs. Pasquale turned to Sue. With a swift passionate gesture she seized her own hair in her good hand and seemed about to tear it out and present it to Sue.

"To-morrow," she said. "You! Come!"

Sue stared at her blankly.

Mrs. Pasquale tried again, scorning the assistance of her interpreter. She let go of her hair and stabbed herself in the head with a forefinger. "You!" she said. Then her face brightened. She tore a braid apart and began to comb through it with an energy which seemed likely to remove every hair from her head.

"You! To-morrow! Come! Yes?"

A great light burst upon Sue.

"Yes," she said. "To-morrow — come. Yes! Of course I'll do your hair."

Mrs. Pasquale seized her in a crushing hug.

"Nize-a girl!" she roared.

V

THE REFORMERS

SUE found the ward a pleasant place now that her difficulty with Mrs. Pasquale had been settled. The patients accepted her placidly, and in a few days she felt as much a part of the ward as if she had been there always.

After the daily strain of classes it was restful to come into the warm, sunny ward and be greeted with smiles; to hurry back and forth with drinks or blankets which were received gratefully and without criticism; to wait on the fringe of the kitchen turmoil for trays; to watch the shadows of the elms lengthening across the lawn and know that as soon as visiting hour was over preparations for the night would begin. There would be tired backs to rub, crumpled bottom sheets to brush and tighten, hot pillows to be turned under hotter cheeks; ice caps and hot water bags to be filled. And there was always Miss Waring, steady-eyed and competent, encouraging with the right word at the right time.

Sue and Hilda practised on the ward the things learned under the awful guidance of Miss Cameron. They progressed from bed making to bed baths, and then to taking temperatures, giving alcohol sponges, making poultices, giving massage, hypodermics, medicines. There seemed no end to it, but it was all interesting.

Dr. Barry made the rounds of the ward daily, but seldom during the hours when Sue was on duty. When she encountered him he smiled at her from the depths of his clear, deep-set eyes, but he seemed very far away, and absorbed in matters far more interesting than a red-headed probationer.

"I love all this, don't you?" Hilda said to Sue one evening as they were walking home to Brewster. All around them the gray and red of the hospital buildings were dim in the autumn dusk. Lights winked in the windows where the night nurses hurried about their work. The wind whispered in the ivy on the old walls.

"Yes," Sue agreed. She couldn't put into words what she felt about the hospital. Hilda was a good sort, she thought, and nice to work with in spite of her worries and glooms and dire predictions. She didn't really mean them.

"You know, Sue," Hilda went on, "you're lucky to have made two friends like Kit and Connie. It must be fun to have chums right from the beginning. I guess we all envy you — except that Francesca Manson."

"Doesn't she like us?" Sue asked. Francesca Manson was the older girl with the hard face who had been so unpleasant to Grace Holton the first night.

"I don't know — exactly. Nobody knows what that girl thinks. She's so hard-boiled, and she makes fun of everything and everybody — especially me."

"Don't pay any attention to her," Sue said absently, and gave the matter no more thought.

She recalled it the next day, however. It was Saturday and all the probationers had the afternoon off. She found Kit and Connie in the living room of Brewster, in earnest conversation.

"I think it's rotten," Kit was saying.

"Well, it isn't just that," Connie interrupted her. "I don't think she minds so much now, but she will if it keeps on because the other girls are beginning to do it, too, and if everybody begins thinking the girl's a fool, she'll begin to think so herself after a while — and that's awful."

"What *are* you ranting about?" Sue demanded as the girls made room for her on the couch.

"We're being righteously indignant about the way Francesca Manson treats Hilda Grayson. Hadn't you noticed it?"

"Well, I haven't seen them together much," Sue said. "We hardly ever go to the same meals." She paused, frowning. "Come to think of it, Hilda did say something about it yesterday."

"I should think she might," Kit said. "The minute poor Hilda comes into the dining room Manson begins. The other kids are getting so they expect it. They egg Manson on, and she simply adores it." Kit snorted. "Goodness knows, you can't prove it by me that Hilda is exactly a genius, but if I were a patient I'd ever so much rather be nursed by her than by dear Francesca."

"What does Manson do?"

"You tell her, Connie. You're good at making long speeches."

"Well," Connie began, "you know the way Manson is — with that lopsided smile that makes her look as if somebody were pinching her?"

"Yes. Go on."

"She starts with that. She looks at Hilda as if the poor kid had just crawled out from under a rock. This noon she inquired how Hilda was doing on the ward — as if, you know, Hilda did awful work. She doesn't, does she?"

"Certainly not. She's very good."

"Hilda's so deadly serious. She said the worst possible thing. Her eyes got all round and earnest and she said she thought the patients were beginning to like her a little."

"The patients love her. Go on."

"And then Manson said, 'That makes everything perfect, doesn't it — but then, of course, I knew the moment I saw you that you were born to be a ray of sunshine. You're such a worthy person, Grayson. It inspires me to have you around.'"

"What a beastly thing to say!" Sue was sincerely shocked.

"Yes, wasn't it! Even Hilda got that. She didn't know what to say. What can you say to that sort of thing?"

"You can't. What happened then?"

"Then Manson turned sympathetic. She leaned across the table and looked Hilda up and down, all over her curves and billows, and said in a shocked voice, 'You poor child — I believe you 're putting on weight.' Everybody simply shouted at that and Hilda got all red and flustered. And still Manson could n't let her alone. She went on in an awful warning tone, 'Let me give you a piece of advice, Grayson. You 'd better watch yourself in Miss Cameron's class. It 's lucky for you that your ward work is improving — but I 'm afraid even that — ' "

"Oh!" Sue cried. "But you can't do things like that to people. It 's cruel."

"You can't — but Manson can. Hilda went as white as a sheet, and said, 'But I have n't done anything!' And Manson said, 'Oh, have n't you? That 's all right then. I guess Miss Cameron was mistaken.' "

"But Hilda has n't done anything, has she?"

"No, of course not. Don't be silly. But she thinks she has now. She looked so frightened it made me a little sick. And when she was going out of the dining room one of Manson's little satellites remarked that if Grayson got any dumber we 'd have to start making signs at her — and peals of girlish laughter echoed through the whole dining room. Hilda heard it, of course. I think it 's dreadful."

"But Hilda is n't in the least dumb. She 's sort of slow, but she gets there in the end. She just means well, and you can't do anything about that. She 's a good

66

kid. I like her. But something ought to be done about Manson."

"What can you do," Kit asked, "beside jumping up and down on her until she says she's sorry?"

"That's not such a bad idea," Sue said. "Only I don't think the hospital would like it."

"I suppose poor old Hilda is up in her room, ending it all."

"Well, she hasn't ended it all yet. Look!"

They turned to follow Sue's glance. Hilda was coming down the corridor in a neat, tailored suit. Her eyes were bright with excitement and her childlike mouth quivered. She lumbered, beaming, into the living room.

"Hello!" she said. "Say, did you know that if you have the afternoon off and first hours in the morning you can spend the night away from the hospital?"

"Why, no," Connie said with her friendly smile. "But wait a minute — yes I did, too. It was posted on the bulletin board our first day. I guess I forgot about it, and so did everyone else. Few of us know people around here, to visit. What are you going to do?"

"I've got an aunt in the suburbs and I'm going out to stay with her — and if anybody says hospital to me while I'm there I'll scream."

"Whom do you have to tell about it?" Sue asked suddenly. She, too, had paid no attention to the notice about overnight permission.

"Just the Training School Office."

"Nobody else knows you're going — none of the girls?"

"Why, no, I haven't seen anybody but you three. Why?"

"Oh, I just wondered."

"Well," said the unsuspicious Hilda, "I've got to hurry. See you to-morrow."

"Good-bye," the three said, and stared at each other behind Hilda's broad, retreating back.

"Are you," said Connie slowly, "thinking what I'm thinking?"

"Something very similar," Kit admitted.

Sue looked at Kit with satisfaction. "It was your saying that about Hilda ending it all — "

"Same here," said Connie. "But how'll we do it?"

"We've got to do it," said Sue. "We've got to have Manson simply gnawing her shoestrings with worry. It's raining out, too. What could be more perfect?"

Connie fell into line. "Poor dear Hilda," she sighed, "wandering out into the storm, despair and self-destruction in her mind. All through the long night she does not return and her persecutor suffers torments of remorse."

Kit chuckled. "Could anything be eleganter! But see here, what about when Hilda pops in again in the morning, having spent a cosy night with her suburban aunt? That's going to be difficult."

"Oh," said Sue carelessly, "I'll take care of that later. The main thing now is to start Manson on her shoestring."

Francesca Manson's room was on the third floor, next door to Grace Holton's. Just across from Grace's room was an ice-water tank. The girls clustered around it, rustling the paper cups noisily.

"Oh, dear, Grace is out," Sue said in a loud voice. "That's too bad. Now we'll have to go without her." And then in a whisper, "Manson's in — look — there's her shadow on the threshold."

Connie faced Francesca's room so that she could be heard distinctly.

"Why don't we ask Hilda Grayson to go to the movies with us, Sue? You know her quite well, and she seems a lonely soul. I'll bet she'd love to go."

"I wish we'd thought of that sooner," said Sue in a gloomy voice. "But it's too late now."

"Why, Sue!" Kit said. "Is there anything the matter?"

"I'm afraid so. Maybe it's all my imagination — but I'm worried. Something has upset her — and she's gone. I didn't want to say anything about it — yet."

"What *do* you mean, Sue?" Connie demanded, stifling a giggle.

"Sh-shh!" Sue lowered her voice. "Somebody might hear us. And if I'm wrong — " She nudged Connie. The shadow on the floor of Francesca's room was tensely still.

"Sue! You look awful! What is it?" Kit implored.

"Well, I'll tell you, but you mustn't breathe a word of it. I tried to stop her, but I couldn't. She may come back — she'll have to be back by ten if she's coming at all — and I might be mistaken. It would be a horrid thing to have get around."

69

"We won't tell a soul!"

"Well, working with Hilda as I do, I've come to know things about her. She's always been subject to fits of depression — I've an idea there's melancholia in the family — and to-day she was in an awful state. She tried to hide it, but *I* know. Of course, she never *said* anything about suicide, but those people are the worst kind."

"Oh, no!" Connie cried, one eye on the motionless shadow.

"I'm very much afraid — " Sue paused and then went on — "she seemed very excited when she left, and she said that if anyone said hospital to her she'd scream. She's very hysterical, you know. I tried to keep her here, but once people like that get an idea you can't do anything with them."

"Ought n't we to go to the office about it?"

"What could they do? Besides, you never can tell about that type. She's gone out into this awful storm and it may bring her to her senses."

"Oh, Sue!" Kit's voice was terrified. "Maybe she left a note. They nearly always do."

"Not necessarily. And anyway — I — I'm afraid to look."

They went away, along the corridor to the elevator.

"There!" Kit said. "That ought to start Francesca down the street on her roller skates."

"I think we've got real talent," Connie said. "If we get thrown out of here we can always go on the stage."

"Shut up," Kit hissed — "and look!"

They drew back into the shadow behind the elevator shaft. It was grilled iron and they could see perfectly without being seen. Francesca was standing in the door of her room, looking up and down the corridor. Her lips were tense. After a moment she stepped out into the corridor and went quickly to the stairs at the other end.

"She's going up to see if there's a note. Come on!"

They ran up the stairs at the end of the corridor and waited at the top, still in the shadow of the elevator.

Francesca approached Hilda's room cautiously, looked back, and then darted inside.

"Make a good porch climber, wouldn't she?" Sue whispered.

"Look out! She'll see you!"

Francesca had come out. Her movements were quick and nervous.

The girls slipped back to the third floor.

"Got her the first time," said Sue, as Francesca's door closed.

"What'll we do now?" Kit asked.

"Let the yeast work," said Sue. "We might as well go to the movies, and then, after dinner, if she's in, we can work on her some more."

Francesca remained in, for the girls saw her in the dining room at dinner, though she sat at another table. About nine o'clock they wandered up to the third floor, past her room. There was no one there.

"She's visiting somewhere around. Let's have a look."

They loitered in the hallways, rambled in and out of

71

rooms, and drank ice water from all the tanks on all the floors, but there was no sign of Francesca.

"For mercy's sake, Sue," Kit said at last. "My tonsils are floating. Can't you think of something to do beside drink water?"

"We might take off our shoes and stockings and wade," Sue suggested. "I wish to goodness she'd turn up so we could tell her some more about Hilda's melancholia."

"Well, could n't we just go and sit down somewhere for a minute?" Kit begged. "I'll have fallen arches if I have to carry this water around much longer."

"Oh, all right — sissy!"

They wandered down to the living room, drawn by the sound of music and the shuffling of feet. The nurses were dancing to the victrola and the room was alive with laughter and rhythm and the cheerful crackling of an open fire. The girls glanced eagerly around the room and there, in a far corner, curled up with a book, was Francesca.

"Ah!" said Sue.

"Why, the heartless wretch!" Connie murmured. "Let's waken her to a sense of responsibility."

They strolled over to the corner and began to examine the books in the bookcase against the wall. Francesca glanced up at them and then dropped her eyes. She seemed completely absorbed in her book.

"Gee! What a ghastly night!" Sue said at last in a melancholy voice, as she shoved a book back into place on the shelves.

Connie moved to the window and looked out. "It's frightful out," she said. "I'd hate to be down around the river to-night, with the wind blowing the way it is. The waves must be well over the Esplanade."

Francesca did not move, but the lines around her mouth deepened.

Kit began to pace back and forth.

"Don't *do* that!" Sue implored. "You make me nervous."

Kit sat down and drummed with her fingers on the arm of her chair.

"I'm sorry," she said, "but I just can't help thinking of — "

"Oh, do be quiet," Sue said sharply.

"If only it weren't raining so," said Connie from the window. She was still looking out at the blurred lights of the hospital.

Inspiration seized her. She drew a deep breath and clasped her hands behind her back. The girls were to come to know that gesture well, but they were seeing it now for the first time.

"Did you ever stand on a bridge at night, in a storm?" Connie said. She spoke breathlessly, raising her voice above the wailing of a jazz record. "The wind roars under the arches, and shrieks through the girders — and blows your wet hair across your face — and the gray parapets have turned all black and shiny and cold — and there's no friendliness anywhere — just howling wind and merciless rain — and you feel cut off from everything —

73

until — when you look down — over the parapet — at the black water raging below — you wonder if it would hurt very much — if — if you jumped — far out, you know — and went down to meet it — " She stopped.

Kit and Sue were staring at her in amazement. Francesca closed her book with a bang, sprang out of her chair, and left the room.

Connie turned away from the window.

"How was I?" she asked.

"You were much too good," Kit said with a shiver. "I'm glad I'm right here where it's nice and warm. But you should have seen her face, Connie. It was the most beautiful, delicate shade of green. Whatever possessed you?"

"I don't know," Connie said seriously. "Something came over me."

"I should think it did!" Sue said briskly. "Well, that's that! I hope she has a pleasant night, filled with the most elegant nightmares. You'd give anybody nightmares, Connie, talking like that."

"Thank you," said Connie, beaming, and the girls stared. Sue's remark had not been intended as a compliment.

"You'd better go to bed, old thing," Kit said. "If you don't you'll begin picking things out of the air and counting your fingers."

They departed from the living room arm in arm, and went upstairs to bed pleasantly conscious of a good piece of work well done. Their sleep was untroubled by any prickings of conscience or worries as to how they would extricate themselves or Hilda from the situation they had created.

Sue was wakened in the morning for a happy moment by the rising bell, and lay listening to the hurried departure to the wards of nurses who did *not* have the morning off. Then she hunched the bedclothes around her shoulders and drifted off into a warm slumber — from which she was aroused by Connie, who stood over her, fully dressed.

"Wake up, Sue! It's nearly eleven o'clock. Manson's been up to Hilda's room, found it empty, and is having a fit. I don't believe she's once thought of overnight permission. She's been walking up and down her room until she must have worn a path in the rug."

Sue sprang out of bed.

"Oh, golly!" she moaned. "It must be almost time for Hilda to come in. How'll we ever keep her from spilling everything all over the place?"

"That's your lookout, my bright little girl," said Kit from the doorway. "I suggested yesterday that we might get into trouble at this point, but you said you'd take care of that."

"Well, it's nice to know I've got such cheerful supporters." Sue paused suddenly in the hasty process of pulling on her clothes. "You don't suppose that Manson would go to the Office, do you?"

"No, I don't," said Connie. "She'd be too scared of starting something she could n't finish, and she'd want to keep out of trouble."

"I hope so. Well, come on."

They ran down the stairs to waylay Hilda at the front door, and they were not a moment too soon. Hilda was coming in as they leaped down the last flight of stairs.

The girls greeted her with enthusiasm, but there was no chance to explain anything. The corridor was swarming with nurses and probationers. Somewhat to Hilda's surprise they escorted her in a body to her room and hovered over her while she changed into uniform. But their luck was gone. A first-year nurse dropped in and sat down comfortably on the bed. She could not be dislodged, and she accompanied them firmly to the dining room.

Sue was thinking fast. She was conscious that Kit and Connie were looking at her sourly, but it was not her fault, she thought bitterly. It was too late now to tell Hilda anything even if there had been a chance to do so. The only hope — and a slim one — lay in the fact that Hilda was obviously very tired. She had not slept well, she told the girls — and she looked it. But that was just what she would tell anyone who inquired how she was.

Sue had meant to arrange some story for Hilda about Francesca so that Hilda would unconsciously make the right replies to anything Francesca might ask her. But it was too late now, and it was useless to tell her the truth. Within two hours she would have let five or six people in on the secret, and once Francesca learned of it she would persecute Hilda mercilessly, in revenge.

The dining room was filling rapidly, and Sue gave a faint moan when she saw that Francesca was ahead of them, and seated, with Lois Wilmont, at the only probationers' table which had any vacancies.

Francesca looked up as the little procession came in, with Hilda in the lead, and her strained features relaxed in an expression of such unutterable relief that Sue felt a sudden and acute pang of remorse.

Hilda approached the table with the slow dignity of a ferry coming in to dock, and sat down heavily.

"Hello, Grayson," Francesca said, very pleasantly.

"Hello," Hilda returned.

"Well, what have you been up to?" The question was asked casually, but Sue noted that Francesca's eyes were bright with curiosity.

"I've been out." Hilda, for once, was guarded. She had been baited once too often.

Sue breathed a sigh of relief.

"Have a good time?"

"Why, y — "

"Hilda's exhausted," Sue put in quickly. She leaned forward to lay a protecting arm along the back of Hilda's chair. "She hasn't slept, and she doesn't want to think — about — I mean, she's very tired."

Hilda's look of surprise did not escape Francesca. Her eyes hardened in a sudden suspicion.

"Where *were* you?" she demanded sharply.

"Why, I — " Hilda began.

"She told you, she's been out," Sue said. "She's been walking, haven't you, Hilda? You did walk, didn't you?"

"Why — why, yes," Hilda said, bewildered. "But —"

"Look here, just what *is* all this?" Francesca asked, in an ominously quiet voice.

"I do think," Sue remarked, "that what Hilda does outside the hospital is her own affair. Apparently nothing that she does inside it is."

"Yes," Kit said, the light of battle in her eye. "Can't she do anything without being cross-questioned, Manson?"

"I do think it's rotten of you, Manson," Connie added.

"I asked a civil and friendly question," Francesca said coldly. "Is there anything the matter with it?"

"There is if she doesn't want to tell you," Connie snapped.

"But —" Hilda tried again. "I don't mind tell —"

"Never mind, Hilda. You don't have to," Sue said. She turned on Francesca. "Hilda's business is her own, Manson, even if you don't seem to think so. Is all this persecution necessary?"

"I wasn't aware," Francesca said stiffly, "that asking a simple, conventional question came under the head of persecution."

"Neither was I," Sue drawled, "until I heard you ask one!"

The situation was getting completely out of hand. What

might have happened next Sue was never to learn, for Lois Wilmont was becoming uneasy. Now she broke into the conversation.

"But Hilda, where were you last night?" she asked. "It 's very ill-bred to be mysterious."

Hilda looked from one face to another, dazed. Sue glanced in desperation at Kit — at Connie. Their faces were impassive. Either they could not, or would not help her. Hilda's mouth opened. In another second it would all be over — or rather the worst would be beginning.

"The truth," Lois said, "is always — "

"Ah!" The exclamation burst from Sue before she realized it. A wave of relief swept over her. Her eyelashes hid the gleam of joy in her eyes for an instant, but when she looked up to meet Lois's stern look, her own was faltering, uncertain.

"There — there is n't anything mysterious about it," she said, and her tone would not have convinced a baby. "Hilda stayed last night with — her aunt — who lives in — in —" she seemed to grope frantically for a name — "in *Rockland!*" she finished triumphantly.

"Really?" said Lois in an incredulous voice.

Hilda was greatly relieved. "Honestly," she said. "I did spend the night with my aunt."

Lois eyed her with scorn, and Hilda's eyes filled with tears. She struggled to her feet.

"I — I won't stay here," she stammered, "and be picked over like — like — a bone." And she fled from the dining room.

With grave faces Kit and Sue and Connie paraded out after her.

"Whew!" Kit exclaimed, once they were outside. "Was that a narrow escape, or are we still hanging in the balance?"

"As far as I'm concerned, I'm still hanging." Sue passed a hand across her forehead. "I don't know whether Manson believed us or not — I mean, disbelieved us or — well —"

"We know what you mean," Connie said. "I couldn't tell a thing by Manson's face. And do you realize that we had no breakfast, and now, in the interests of drama, we've missed our lunch. I'm ravenous!"

"So'm I!" Kit said.

Sue made no reply. She was wondering how to straighten things out in Hilda's mind.

During the first ten or fifteen minutes on the ward she had no chance to speak to Hilda, who, with swollen eyes, was putting away laundry in the linen closet.

At the first opportunity Sue hurried out, determined to tell Hilda the truth and trust to luck that she wouldn't give the whole thing away. A sound of low voices stopped her before she reached the linen-closet door.

"It doesn't matter," Hilda was saying.

Another voice — Francesca's — spoke earnestly. "But it does matter, Grayson, really. You might at least listen, because if I'm caught over here I'll get into trouble. I didn't mean to be prying, and I'm terribly sorry. I've been rather nasty to you — for no reason at all, and I've been worrying about it ever since — er — ever since last night. No — you need n't tell me about that — I know. I did n't mean what I said about Miss Cameron. I was just teasing. I meant to have told you at the table, but those three devils would n't give me a chance."

Sue tiptoed back into the ward.

"Well, I 'll be a monkey's uncle!" she whispered to herself.

VI

JUSTICE AND THERMOMETERS

AFTER this things settled down to a quiet routine which was broken briefly by the Hallowe'en Masquerade at Grafton Hall. Even Miss Cameron's classes were comparatively uneventful. In spite of that, however, the probationers were increasingly nervous. Two months of their probation were gone. There was only one more to go. A girl in Sue's section left the hospital suddenly, saying that she was tired of it. Two others were called to the office, from which they returned red-eyed, packed their trunks, and departed, giving no explanation. But as their work had been consistently poor from the beginning the class, though frightened by this, was not surprised.

Sue had not seen Dr. Barry for some time, and one morning when she was busy in the laboratory she was startled to hear his voice in the passageway.

"Don't bother about me, Miss Waring," he was saying. "I know you're busy. Lend me one of your probationers. They can surely do dressings by this time."

"Well — if you don't mind," Miss Waring answered. "They're good, both of them. Let's see — Miss Grayson has gone to the apothecary. And Miss Barton — where —

Oh! there you are! Miss Barton, will you help Dr. Barry with Miss Coleman's dressing, please."

Sue had learned how to change dressings in Miss Cameron's class, but she had not had much chance for practice on the ward, as the dressings were usually all done by the time she arrived from class — except those saved to be done by the probationers under strict supervision. She had never done one with a doctor, and she knew that Dr. Barry was watching her with amused eyes as she inspected the dressing tray.

"You're getting up in the world, are n't you?" he remarked, as she set the tray down on the patient's table and drew a screen around the bed. "How do you like nursing, now?"

"Ever so much," Sue answered seriously. Miss Cameron's instructions rang in her ears as she turned the bedclothes down to the patient's waist and laid the sterile towel containing the surgical instruments on the folds, exactly as she had been taught. She removed the safety pins from the dressing, opened a package of gauze sponges, and dropped them on the opened sterile towel. Then she set a pail on the floor and stood waiting.

"Very nice," Dr. Barry commented. He lifted the stained gauze from the dressing with a pair of forceps and dropped it in the pail. "Now, Miss Coleman — this will take just a minute."

Miss Coleman stirred apprehensively.

"Oh, Doctor, are you going to take out the stitches?"

"You won't mind it at all, Miss Coleman," Sue said

quickly. "They don't hurt when they're taken out properly." She laid a warm, reassuring hand on Miss Coleman's thin one. For an instant Sue felt that she was not herself, but Miss Coleman. She could feel the weight of the bedclothes on her feet, the smoothness of the sheet beneath her, the tiredness of lying in bed for a long time, and the stir of apprehension at the thought of stitches, and she looked down at the woman with such a warmth of understanding that Miss Coleman's fingers tightened gratefully about her hand. Dr. Barry was watching her.

"You do like it, don't you?" he said.

"Yes."

There was silence for a few minutes. Dr. Barry's fingers were quick and gentle and presently Miss Coleman relaxed with a sigh. Sue was ready with a basin of alcohol and more sponges. As the stitches came out, one by one, with a snip of the scissors and a sure movement of the forceps, Dr. Barry talked to the patient, asking an occasional question, teasing her a little. Miss Coleman lay quiet, looking up at him with perfect confidence.

When the dressing was finished and the bedclothes straightened, Sue took the instruments out to the sterilizer. Dr. Barry followed her.

"That was very nicely done, Miss Barton," he said. "I think you've chosen the right profession. You should make a good operating nurse."

Sue flushed with pleasure.

"Thank you," she said. "But how can you tell? Anybody can do a simple dressing."

He leaned back against the window casing and surveyed her.

"It is n't what one does, but how one does it. You 're very quick, but it 's the quickness of intelligence, and not of nervousness." And then, abruptly, "Your probation is nearly done, is n't it?"

"Yes."

"I suppose you 're full of qualms?"

"Yes, awfully."

"Don't be — you 're all right."

"But Miss Cameron — "

He laughed. "She 's a grand old girl. You 've nothing to fear from her. She 's the incarnation of Justice."

"That 's what Miss Waring says. But it — it 's a little hard to realize just now. She terrifies us so, and she 's so hard to please, and really and truly she *is* unreasonable. I don't think it 's just to be unreasonable. She expects impossible things of us — and I wish she 'd have a little human weakness once in a while."

"That 's just it. She expects the impossible — and you accomplish it — don't you?"

Sue looked at him, startled. "Why — why, yes," she said slowly. "I believe we do. We think we can't, and we can. I 'd never thought of it like that."

"There you are. And when you come up against a really difficult situation with her, you 'll find that she 's both human and fair. She does n't really expect the impossible. She merely expects the utmost of which you are capable."

85

"How do you know so much about Miss Cameron?"
His eyes twinkled.

"Well," he confided, "I'd heard about her — one does, you know. And then one day I saw her going through a corridor like an Avenging Fate, and I thought she'd be worth knowing. So I called on her. We're quite good friends now. She's splendid!"

Sue thought this over a good many times in the course of the morning, and wished that she could see Miss Cameron in that light. It would help a lot. Perhaps she would, some day.

That day, however, seemed very remote. And the very next morning in class Miss Cameron seemed bent upon justifying Sue's doubts and proving Dr. Barry mistaken. She had never been more difficult. Before the class had been in session fifteen minutes the probationers were in a dripping perspiration from nervousness.

It was Miss Cameron's custom to lecture to the class on the subject to be taken up that day, explaining every move, and giving a list of the equipment required. After this she gave a personal demonstration of the procedure, using Mary Chase, the rubber doll, as the patient. The class no longer found Mary Chase funny. They envied her. She couldn't make mistakes.

When the demonstration was finished the class had overnight to study their notes. The next day Miss Cameron called upon some member of the class to come up on the platform and go through the demonstration again, explaining as she went along. A single item of equipment forgotten, a single move made at the wrong time, brought down all Miss Cameron's wrath on the unhappy probationer.

She began, that morning, by calling on Grace Holton to make a flaxseed poultice. There was a cold look in her eyes which the class knew meant trouble. Grace, after one stealthy peek at her notes, rushed from the room to get the poultice equipment. Miss Cameron's eyes followed her with a dreadful intensity.

"The other section must have done something idiotic," Kit whispered to Sue.

Miss Cameron pounced instantly.

"Well, Miss Van Dyke!"

Kit stared, paralyzed, unable to think of any reasonable reply to this.

"Speak up!"

"I — nothing, Miss Cameron."

"*Nothing!* This is not a social gathering, Miss Van Dyke. You are here to learn — if you are able to do so. If you have any remarks to make, please make them to me." Her jaws closed with an audible snap.

"Y-yes, Miss Cameron."

Grace returned, wild-eyed, carrying her equipment, which Miss Cameron inspected with the manner of one expecting to find a murderer concealed in it.

"What are you waiting for! Begin!"

Grace, with shaking hands, began to make the flaxseed poultice, and Miss Cameron's silent watching held the class spellbound. The smell of cooking flaxseed spread through the warm classroom. The silence was broken only by Grace's quavering voice explaining what she was doing. Miss Cameron sat motionless, her eyes on Grace's hands. When the poultice was finished Grace gave one feebly hopeful glance at Miss Cameron, who seemed about to spring at her. Grace gathered up her equipment and fled.

Miss Cameron addressed the class. "We will have another demonstration, of the hot-air bath." Her eyes searched the apprehensive faces before her and came to rest on Kit, who grew visibly smaller.

"Miss Van Dyke will give the demonstration. Miss Wilmont will be subject. Go to your room, Miss Wilmont, and change to your night clothes and bathrobe. Quickly!"

Lois and Kit rose together, and left the room, Lois smug with relief and Kit with the alacrity born of fear.

No probationer was allowed to refer to her notes in collecting the equipment for a demonstration. She must remember everything. Kit was gone a long time. Sue and Connie dared not look at each other. They sat in miserable suspense. Lois had returned, beaming — being subject for a demonstration entailed no difficulties. Miss Cameron's look at Kit, when she finally appeared, was withering.

The demonstration began smoothly enough. Lois got into bed and drew up the covers. Kit, having arranged her equipment as prescribed, covered Lois with a blanket, drew the bedclothes back from under it, and placed a large wooden framework known as a "cradle" on the bed.

This held the clothes high above the body of the patient, making a sort of cave. Two blankets went over this and were tucked in around Lois's shoulders so that no hot air should escape. The ends of the blanket were left free at the foot of the bed.

It was then that Kit paused in consternation. She had forgotten the large rubber sheet which came next. Miss Cameron's expression was ominous. Kit dashed from the room and returned with the rubber sheet, which she put on the cradle over the two blankets. Two other blankets followed this, and in the relief afforded by continual activity Kit was beginning to gain confidence.

"What's this?"

Kit straightened up. Miss Cameron was glaring at a five-pint bottle of bichloride of mercury which stood on the table with the other things.

"I—I meant to have brought the alcohol, Miss Cameron."

"Meant! Meant! You don't know what you mean! Nurses cannot make mistakes! There is no place in the profession for young women who do not know what they are doing!"

Kit went over to the table and picked up the offending bottle with an instinctive desire to get rid of it somewhere — anywhere.

"Miss Van Dyke!"

Kit started. The heavy bottle slipped from her hand and crashed to the platform. In the awful silence which followed the blue bichloride trickled along the platform and dripped over the edge onto the floor in a widening pool. Kit and the class stared at it, fascinated.

"Get the mop!"

Kit's feet took her mechanically from the room and brought her back again with the mop. Somehow the floor was cleaned and the broken glass removed.

"Don't cut yourself!" Miss Cameron said once, sharply, but that was all.

Kit went on with the demonstration scarcely knowing what she did. Her every move was willed in advance by the intensely concentrated class. At last the little alcohol stove with its angular asbestos pipe was in place at the foot of the bed. The blankets were tucked in around it, and with trembling fingers Kit knelt and lit a match. The wick refused to catch. She lit another, and another, until Miss Cameron grimly took the box of matches from her hand and lit one herself. But even she had no effect on the stubborn wick.

The class remained outwardly grave. Inwardly they were one broad and united smile.

At last Miss Cameron snatched the spirit lamp from its place, shook it, unscrewed the top, and sniffed.

"*Rubbing* alcohol!" she thundered. She turned on Kit. "Did you fill this, Miss Van Dyke?"

"N-no, Miss Cameron. It — it was a-already full," Kit stammered in her eagerness to disclaim any connection with the stove.

"Take it out and fill it with the proper alcohol!"

Her glare pierced Kit's retreating shoulder blades.

When Kit returned the lamp submitted peaceably to being lighted. An ice cap was placed on Lois's head. Miss Cameron stepped forward and reached under the blankets to look at the bath thermometer. It was not there.

The class sat transfixed with horror.

Miss Cameron ignored Kit as one unworthy of further notice.

"Miss Barton, get the thermometer, please."

A cold hand clutched at the pit of Sue's stomach. She rose to her feet trying desperately to remember where the thermometer was kept. It would never do to appear uncertain. Some instinct led her to the classroom closet. She opened the door with an assured manner, praying that the thermometer would be there. The class craned their necks after her. Miss Cameron waited, stony-eyed.

The thermometer was not there.

She had looked in the wrong place. Miss Cameron would know, now, that Sue had no idea where the thermometer was kept, but at least one could keep up a front a little longer. The only other possible places to look would be the laboratory or the linen closet. Sue hurried out, ransacked the shelves in both places, and found no thermometer.

There was nothing to do but go back and admit that she did n't know where it was.

Sue stopped in the classroom doorway feeling as though it were a guillotine.

"I — I can't find it, Miss Cameron!"

"Bring me that thermometer at once!"

Sue fled back to the laboratory and tried to collect her wits. Where was Miss Cameron's famous justice now? Let Dr. Barry explain this if he could. The thermometer was not in its proper place, wherever that might be. Sue had not put it away, but she was expected to produce it instantly. How could you produce something which wasn't?

In a frenzy of nervousness Sue pulled down everything on the laboratory shelves, left the things on the floor, and ran to the linen closet. She tugged at sheets, blankets, boxes. They all came down at once.

The thermometer was not there and that was that.

Regardless of the disorder she was leaving behind her, Sue returned to the classroom. The stiff white figure on the platform was waiting for her with eyes which were two points of polished steel. There was nothing left in all the world but those and the class, which was a blur of staring faces.

"It isn't there, Miss Cameron," Sue managed at last.

Miss Cameron rose from her chair and took three steps forward to the edge of the platform.

"You are a disgrace to the profession, Miss Barton. It is the business of a nurse to know where all equipment is kept. Your behavior is very strange. I have told you to bring me the bath thermometer. You have failed to do so. I cannot have you in my class. You will remain outside until the end of the session. I will see you then."

"Yes, Miss Cameron."

Sue turned on her heel and went out. What now? Well, she could pick up the things she had strewn on the floor. It was while she was putting the laboratory in order that Grace Holton appeared at her elbow, breathless.

"Barton! She's sent me for the thermometer and she's furious. What'll I do? I don't know where it's supposed to be."

"It isn't here," Sue said dully. "Don't waste your time looking. Go back and tell her."

Grace scurried back to the classroom, and Sue was alone again with Miss Cameron's words ringing in her ears. "I cannot have you in my class —" Did that mean always? Would she be packing her trunk to-night, to leave this place which was now her world? Would she never again see the sunny ward with its rows of white beds? Sue caught her breath and her eyes stung.

"Barton! She's thrown me out of class, too!"

It was Grace, with wide frightened eyes. Sue pulled herself together.

"Well, welcome to my midst. You might as well help me clear up this mess."

They worked silently and Sue, looking up once, saw that Grace was crying. The linen closet was nearly in order when another probationer burst in upon them.

"I'm after the thermometer," she moaned. "Where is it?"

"That's a bright question to ask *us*," Sue said bitterly.

The probationer clambered, panting, up the linen-

93

closet shelves, dropped to the floor and dashed out. She returned almost instantly.

"I'm out of class, too," she said.

The situation was beginning to be fantastic. Sue laughed hysterically and even Grace managed a grin.

Connie was next, and after her came Hilda. One by one disgraced probationers gathered in the little entry between the laboratory and the linen closet. There were no less than eleven, now, nearly the entire section. Francesca Manson was the latest. Her celebrated poise was gone beyond recall.

"Golly, girls!" she quavered. "Miss Cameron's as white as a sheet. Wha-what *do* you think she's going to do to us?"

"Whatever it is," Sue said, "she'll have to come out here to do it. She can't do anything to an empty classroom."

"B-but," Hilda wailed, "she still has Kit and Willie, and W-willie's in *bed!*"

A step grated on the concrete and Kit appeared.

"You are all to come back in," she gasped. "Miss Cameron has something to say to you — especially Sue."

Sue's mouth opened and closed again. She was beyond speech.

The probationers filed back into the classroom looking as if they might leap shrieking into the air if anyone touched them or said "Boo!"

Miss Cameron was waiting on the platform.

When everyone was seated she began to speak in a quiet

voice, her eyes returning to Sue from time to time. The listening class sat stunned, unable to believe their ears.

"The thermometer has been found. It was in the drawer of my table. Some careless and stupid young woman from one of the other sections must have left it there. I shall find out who did it."

She paused, and the class shuddered inwardly, thinking of what awaited the unsuspecting probationer who had last had the thermometer.

"I feel," Miss Cameron went on, "that I owe all of you an apology — but most of all Miss Barton. I judged you hastily, Miss Barton, and unfairly. I am very sorry indeed."

She turned to the class again.

"I hope you will profit by this lesson. Some of you have hasty tempers like myself. You will see from this how much distress can be caused by such a weakness. The thermometer should have been in the closet where Miss Barton first looked. She knew where it should have been kept. It was not her fault that some careless person misplaced it, but to-day has been — trying — both for myself and for you. I jumped stupidly at the conclusion that Miss Barton was not keeping her mind on what she was doing, and had simply overlooked the thermometer. I ask your pardon, Miss Barton."

Sue could contain herself no longer. She raised her hand.

"Yes, Miss Barton?" Miss Cameron's voice was gentle.

"Miss Cameron, I — I *did n't* know where it should have been. At least I was n't certain. I 'm very sorry."

95

Miss Cameron's eyes softened as she looked at Sue's flushed face.

"I'm sure you are, Miss Barton. It was very — courageous — of you to own up. I appreciate it. That is all. Class dismissed."

"She was gorgeous," Sue told Dr. Barry later. She had hurried to catch him before he left the ward. "You were so very right, Dr. Barry. I — it made me want to cry. She stood up there before us all and — and humbled herself. And she need n't have, you know."

Dr. Barry stood looking out of the window for a moment before he replied. "No," he said at last, softly, "she need n't have — but she would."

VII

CAPS

THE thing which made probation the most difficult, Sue sometimes thought, was the blue uniform.

"It simply labels you 'inexperienced,'" she said to Kit and Connie. "The nurses are lovely to us, but they're always waiting with their fingers crossed for us to make a mess of something. New patients look nervous when we do anything for them, and the doctors just don't see us at all when they want something. I'll be so thankful when probation's over."

"I shan't," said Kit. "It would be one thing if we were sure of being kept on, but there's always the pleasant chance of finding ourselves standing outside the hospital without any uniforms — blue or otherwise."

"Don't!" Connie implored.

"It would be such an anticlimax," Kit went on relentlessly. "Here we go gayly off to be nurses, prepared to soothe every fevered brow within miles, and the hospital says not any to-day, thank you, and back we go. I don't care how long probation lasts."

"It's funny," Connie said, "how much those caps mean. They look like tin cans turned upside down, and they're

97

as unbecoming as any headgear I ever saw, and yet we yearn after them to the point of frenzy."

Kit and Sue nodded.

What Connie had said was literally true. The little crinoline cap was the climax and the reward of three months of desperate endeavor. To be able to wear it was more important than anything else in the world.

Sue found herself more and more inclined to dreams of the day when she and Hilda should come on the ward, wearing for the first time the hard-earned cap. She refused to admit the possibility that that day might never come — that she might, instead, be going home.

She was shocked and dismayed on the morning when Miss Waring, returning from answering the telephone, said gently, "I'm afraid we're going to lose you, Miss Barton."

Sue's fingers closed tightly on a bedspread. The color drained from her face. All the doubts and fears she had so sternly repressed shouted together in her mind.

"What's happened?"

"My dear child, don't look like that! I'm so sorry. I didn't think. You're not being sent home. You're to report to Ward 7 for duty at once."

"Oh!" Sue gasped. But this was almost as bad. She must leave 23, now so familiar, and go to a strange ward where no one knew her, where she must make a place for herself all over again. Dear old Ward 23. Sue had an absurd desire to clasp it in her arms.

"I'm so sorry, Miss Waring," she cried.

"So am I, Miss Barton. But you must have medical experience before the end of your probation, you know. You can't put in all your time on a surgical ward."

"But I did so want to get my cap on your ward — if I get it at all."

"Come over and let us see it, anyway."

"Oh, may I?" Sue said eagerly I'd love to!"

She said good-bye to the ward, feeling, this time, very much as if she were "going out into the world."

Mrs. Pasquale escorted her to the door, a little dim as to what was happening, but understanding that Sue was going away, somewhere.

"Good-a-bye, nize girl."

"Good-bye, Mrs. Pasquale," Sue said softly, and closed the door on Ward 23.

Her first impression of Ward 7 was of high white walls, a subdued confusion, and an atmosphere of depression. It was strange to see only men patients, to hear gruff voices coming from the beds. And there were no baths to give here. Orderlies did all that kind of work.

The men seemed very morose as compared to the women on 23. Sue was puzzled by it. She had not yet learned that a ward reflects accurately the character of its head nurse.

Ward 7's head nurse was a young graduate with a hawk nose and cold blue eyes, very conscious of the authority of her new white uniforms.

Her first words to Sue were: "Mercy! Another probationer! Things are difficult enough without that."

"She's as warm and comforting as an executioner's axe," Sue told Connie. For, to Sue's delight, Connie also had been sent to Ward 7, and in the sunny quiet of the laboratory where Connie was making soap solution, and Sue had been sent to clean up the place generally, they had a chance to compare notes.

"She isn't sure of herself, and she's afraid somebody will find it out," Connie said shrewdly.

"Of course! I never thought of that."

Connie's penetration often startled Sue, who was not given to analyzing personalities.

Connie stripped the clinging soap from her fingers and held her hands under the cold-water faucet. They were very white, well-kept hands. Her eyes began to twinkle.

"My dear," she said, "you should have been here for the staff visit. It was too marvelous!"

"Oh, what! Do tell me." Sue suspended operations and sat down on the edge of the bathtub. The staff visit on Ward 23 had not been at all exciting. A surgeon came in accompanied by one, or perhaps two, house officers, spoke to Miss Waring, who rose to make the rounds with him, looked at the sicker patients, gave an order or two, and went out.

"You'd think it was royalty, here," Connie grinned. "The Great Man came in — he's a tiny little thing with his hair parted in the middle — followed by *eight* H.O.'s carrying huge case histories. Miss Hackett leaped out of her chair in a perfect frenzy of graciousness. You should have seen her."

Sue laughed. "I'd love to!"

"And, my dear, he did n't so much as look at her — just pointed his cunning little nose at the ceiling and said — " she paused.

"Oh, *do* go on!"

"He said just one little word — but with the manner of a person whose least whisper must be heard around the world — just one little word, without any others before or after, to help it out, you know." Connie's voice quivered.

"Please, Connie!"

"He looked at the ceiling and said — 'Soup!'"

"What?"

"Soup, dear. You know — you drink it."

"If you 're kidding me — " Sue began.

"No. Honestly, Sue. He looked at the ceiling and said 'Soup,' and all the house officers towered around him looking hushed and urgent, and Miss Hackett said, 'Yes, sir, yes, sir, it is all ready.' And if you'll believe it, in came one of the nurses from the kitchen carrying a bouillon cup covered with a napkin, as if it were the crown jewels."

"Oh, *no,* Connie!"

"Oh, yes. But did she put it in his sacred hands? She did not. She was too lowly to come so close to the Presence. She set it on the chimney mantel where he could get it. The only thing that surprised me was that the H.O.'s did n't all kneel while he drank it."

"But why — "

"I 'm sure I don't know. When he had glorified the soup he went around the ward and spent ages with every patient, and made speeches to the H.O.'s. I liked that part," she added honestly. "He was perfectly marvelous when he began talking about diseases. There are some awfully interesting cases on this ward. I was thrilled to death. We 're going to learn a lot here."

"Are you talking about the Emperor Jones?" said a voice behind them.

Sue and Connie turned and Sue rose hastily to her feet. Ward 7's senior was standing in the passageway.

"I can tell you what 's the matter with him," she said with an odd look at Connie. "He 's got a terror of a wife. This is the only place where he can get any respect. I suppose it goes to his head a little. But we don't mind. And he does know an awful lot."

She dropped an armful of laundry in a bag and went out.

"The poor little soul," Connie said. "But what a glorious place a hospital is for henpecked doctors."

She had finished her soap solution, and now she hurried back to the ward, leaving Sue alone to ponder on the odd look the senior had given Connie. She was not the first nurse to do so, and Sue recalled that Connie's own classmates were distant with her. What was the matter with everybody? They acted as if Connie were some kind of strange animal from which anything could be expected. And Connie was such a dear.

Sue decided to get to the bottom of the matter, and it was not long before she had more to think about, though there was still no explanation. She noticed that the nurses, without exception, were polite to Connie, but they did n't joke with her, or tease her. When Sue did a piece of work well or badly there were plenty of comments on it and she got a great deal of unsolicited advice. But no one commented on Connie's work except Miss Hackett, who did so with a studied impartiality. It was obvious that the patients liked Connie, and so did the house officers, who went out of their way to say good-morning to her. But the nurses remained aloof.

At last Sue could stand it no longer. Connie was much too quick not to be aware of this attitude, and though she never mentioned it, Sue suspected that she was unhappy about it. Something ought to be done.

"Why don't any of you like Connie Halliday?" she asked the dish nurse one afternoon, when she and Sue were amiably setting up trays together in the hot little kitchen.

"She's all right," said the dish nurse, noncommittally, and slid another tray onto the pile, with what seemed to Sue unnecessary force.

"But there *is* something," Sue persisted. "Everyone treats her as if she were an outsider and would never be anything else. I wish you'd tell me why."

The dish nurse hesitated, and then said, "All right. I'll tell you. But mind, I'm not criticizing her. She does her work — so far. But we've seen her kind too often to be impressed."

"What do you mean?"

"I mean — these rich society girls. Nursing doesn't really mean anything to them. They just come here for the thrill without intending to stay, or else they really mean to stay until they find that they have to work like anybody else — and that nursing isn't just putting rosebuds in finger bowls. Then they leave, and go back home and laugh at us."

"But Connie isn't like that at all," Sue said hotly. "She wouldn't leave here for anything. She adores it. And you've said, yourself, that her work is all right. I don't think it's fair."

"Well, you wait and see if I'm not right. She won't last long. Do you think she cares anything about this hospital? She does not. That kind always see it as a kind of romantic background for themselves. And I — we — the rest of us don't look at it that way. We growl and grumble about the old place, but we're crazy about it. The hospital isn't us — we are the hospital, if you get me."

"Of course I get you. I feel that way myself. And so does Connie. You'll see. She's got more feeling for this place than you'd ever imagine."

The dish nurse laughed.

Sue told Kit about this later.

"It's so unfair," she said. "They might give her a chance before they lump her with all the others."

"They are giving her a chance, in a way," Kit said slowly. "They're just waiting to be shown, and Connie'll show them in time."

"But can't we do something? If they once realized what the hospital means to Connie — why, it — it's her mother —" Sue stopped, embarrassed.

"I know." Kit, too, was embarrassed. "But we can't do anything. Leave it to Connie."

Sue was reluctantly compelled to admit that Kit was right. It was Connie's own battle. No one could really help her. Besides, it was difficult to worry about anyone but oneself at present. The fatal day which marked the end of probation was drawing near.

Sue was not greatly concerned about the examinations. They were just one more ordeal to endure before the suspense should be over, and she knew that no particular stress was placed on the result of the examinations. One's general work and one's character were what counted. The fifteenth of November would settle everything.

Examination day arrived and the probationers went through it with dogged patience, even though taking Miss Cameron's examination meant having an audience of supervisors. The class knew a faint thrill of pride when it was reported that a house officer, on being shown the questions in anatomy and physiology, had remarked, "Gosh, I don't believe a second-year medical student could pass that."

But what good was having a hard theory exam if its reward was not to be a cap?

The last week dragged interminably. The probationers tried to appear nonchalant, but they were wan and hollow-eyed. The nurses were sympathetic.

"Don't be silly — of course you'll get your cap! Why, I remember — "

But the nurses were not running the Training School Office. Miss Matthews, encountered on rare occasions in the corridors, smiled pleasantly at the blue uniforms, but that was all.

The house officers seemed universally possessed of devils.

"Well! Well!" they said, with hearty cheer. "I suppose you'll be leaving us soon." Or, "Never mind, your family will be glad to have you home again."

The fifteenth of November was cold and gray. By ten o'clock it was raining, a steady, slanting rain, blurring the outlines of the hospital and the bare elms on the lawns. A wet sweet wind flung in gusts against the windows. The gutters streamed and the eaves dripped. In the darker of the hospital corridors electric lights still burned.

The probationers' hearts were as gray as the morning. They went straight to their wards from breakfast. Their classes were over. They performed the tasks given them, but with mechanical precision, and their eyes were glazed. They started when spoken to, and gave very strange replies to questions.

It seemed to Sue that never, since she had been in the hospital, had the ward telephone rung so persistently — with requests to send the patient So-and-So to X-ray, with inquiries about other patients, with demands for someone to come to the apothecary's. And every time the telephone rang it rang through every nerve in Sue's body.

There it was again.

"Ward 7, Miss Hackett speaking. . . . Yes . . . certainly . . . at once."

The same old formula. But *no!*

"Miss Halliday, will you go to the Training School Office, please?"

Connie set an ice-water pitcher carefully on a chair and turned half around. Her lips were white.

"Thank you, Miss Hackett."

She flung one piteous glance at Sue and then walked steadily to the door, but Sue noticed that she groped for the knob. The door closed behind her.

The patients, deeply interested, looked at Sue with one accord, and Sue went on blindly making beds. Of course Connie would get her cap. There could n't possibly be any doubt about it. She *must* get it. She loved the hospital so — no matter what the nurses thought.

Sue moved on to the next empty bed and stripped off the crumpled bedclothes. When it was almost remade she allowed herself to glance at the clock. Connie had been gone twenty minutes! Nothing serious could have happened — certainly not.

Sue did n't hear the door open, but she did hear the ripple of excitement around the ward, and looked up quickly.

Connie was coming down the ward, between the beds, looking very little and very proud. Her eyes shone and her mouth quivered. But Sue did n't see that. She saw only one thing.

Connie was wearing a cap.

"Attaboy, Miss Halliday!"

"Oh, look at our new nurse — she 's a real one, now!"

"Congratulations, Miss Halliday!"

Connie's eyes met Sue's briefly, and then Miss Hackett was shaking her hand. Connie was flushed and laughing as she came to Sue.

"Oh, Connie, I 'm so glad!"

Connie gripped her hand for a moment. "I know you are, old thing. Thanks awfully." She sobered. "Oh, Sue! Margaret Pearson is leaving, and so is that thin blonde girl in the first section. They told Margaret she was too young. They said she had better wait two years and then come back. I don't know why the other one is leaving. She has n't told anybody."

"How dreadful! The poor kids! But Kit — has she — "

"Yes! She 's got it. And so has Hilda — " Connie broke off suddenly. Sue's red head was so conspicuously bare.

They returned silently to their work. Outside, the rising wind moaned around the eaves and shook the windows. Sue's hands were cold, squeezing oranges in the kitchen — the foolish, inconvenient kitchen where everybody stepped on everybody else. How nice to be there, still a part of it. New kitchens were to be built soon. How nice it would be to see them.

But what if one were never again to hurry over the old ward floor, worn to unevenness by the feet of nurses through so many years — nor ever to see the rows of beds all neat and white — nor feel the warm air stirring against one's face — nor to be busy and interested and happy, while outside the cold rain drummed with innumerable fingers on red brick and granite and glistening ivy. Sue's throat tightened.

The door from the ward opened with a rush.

"Training School Office, Miss Barton."

"Yes, Miss Hackett."

All Sue's tenseness stopped with the words. She felt nothing but a kind of tiredness. Her feet carried her down the stairs and along the corridors and across the rotunda. The sight of the Training School Office door gave her a slightly cold feeling, but that was all.

As usual, four pairs of eyes looked her over. But this time a fifth pair was added to them, for Miss Matthews stood beside one of the desks, a pile of fresh white caps at her elbow. Her eyes were very kind.

"Come in, Miss Barton."

Sue stepped over the threshold.

Without another word, but smiling broadly, Miss Matthews selected one of the caps, and before Sue had time fully to realize the significance of that movement she felt a light touch on her head.

Miss Matthews, herself, was pinning the cap in place.

"There, Miss Barton. It looks very nice. Congratulations!"

"I — I — " Sue stammered.

"It's all right, Miss Barton. We know exactly how you feel. It gives me a great deal of satisfaction to tell you that your work has been excellent and that we are very glad to have you in the school. You stand second in your theory class — Miss Wilmont is first — and Miss Cameron has a very high opinion of you. I hope you will be able to maintain this high standard as long as you are in the school."

The shock was almost too much. To Sue's horror she felt her eyes filling with tears. She made a great effort and rescued her self-command.

"Thank you very much, Miss Matthews. I — I am very proud."

"That's splendid. And now — you have an appointment in the sewing room at two o'clock, to be measured for your gray uniforms. That's all, Miss Barton."

Sue's feet barely touched the floor as she sped back through the corridors. House officers and nurses who were total strangers called congratulations after her as she passed them. Everybody seemed to understand. Sue put up her hand. It was really there. It was hers for always. She would go to 23 first and show Miss Waring. At the head of the stairs leading to Ward 23 she met Miss White, who pounded her on the back, and then added a disappointing bit of news: "Miss Waring's off duty."

Sue's face fell. She returned to Ward 7 absurdly disappointed, but no disappointment could last long to-day. Ward 7 made a great fuss over her, and by the time everyone had shaken hands with her and assured her that they knew all the time that she'd get it, her spirits were soaring once more.

On her way to lunch she was unable to resist the temptation to run over to her room and look at herself in the long mirror over her bureau.

She burst in at the door and ran across the room. What was this? Somebody had been here. Sue picked up the object on the bureau. It was a tiny calling card, and around it, wrapped tightly, was an inch-wide band of black velvet — the broad black band worn only by graduate nurses. Sue unwrapped it quickly and saw, written on the card : —

> *To be worn three years from now!*
> *Congratulations.*
> E. M. WARING

"Oh!" Sue said weakly. And then, "What a lovely thing to do. The darling!"

She folded the broad black band with respectful fingers and put it carefully away in her handkerchief box. Three years from now she would take it out again, and it would never go back. She knew that now — as Miss Waring had known all along.

VIII

AND THE GREATEST OF THESE

It had been snowing since the afternoon before, a soft windless snowfall that covered roofs and lawns with unbroken white. Sue's breath on the windowpane melted the delicate mist of frost to an icy transparence as she stared out at the dimly looming wards. Behind her the room was silent except for an occasional rustle when Kit turned another page of her book.

"What do you think she's up to?" Sue said at last, turning to face the placid figure on the bed.

"Gosh, I don't know," Kit mumbled, her eyes glued to her book.

Sue crossed the room in two strides and pounced.

"Hey!" Kit roared, struggling to sit up. "Look out for my cap!"

"Well, pay attention to me then! Did you ask her what she was doing?"

Kit's feet struck the floor with a thump. She reached up and felt tenderly for her cap.

"Yes, I did."

"Well?"

"A lot of satisfaction I got. She said she was concentrating and she went right on walking up and down with her hands behind her back."

"Hm." Sue paused to glance into the mirror and enjoy the slight pleasurable shock of seeing herself in gray and white instead of blue and white. "If she's doing that," she continued, "then she *is* up to something. I suppose we'll just have to wait and find out."

Kit stood up and reached for her apron, which lay neatly folded across the desk.

"One of the things I like about you, Sue," she remarked amiably, "is that you aren't curious — you just want to know."

"My pal!" Sue grinned. "Come on. We'd better get back on duty. Here's your cape."

The warm corridor was intersected at intervals by spots of cold air which seeped out from under night nurses' doors. Sue wrapped the short, gray woolen cape more closely about her.

"Brrr!" she said. "Why didn't we go to the South Seas to train? Shall we go outside or underground?"

"Oh, outside. A little fresh air will do you good."

"You're such a darling, Kit. Always thinking of others."

It was Kit's turn to grin. At the door of Connie's room they stopped to listen to the sound of pacing feet and a faint muttering. Once an exasperated "No!" came to them distinctly.

The girls stared at each other.

"For heaven's sake!" Sue whispered.

Kit shook her head and they went on down the corridor.

"She'll have to tell us sooner or later," Sue said.

But she was mistaken. Connie told them nothing. She was absent-minded off duty and in class, and as Christmas approached she became more and more distraught. Twice on the ward Sue found her in earnest conversation with young Dr. Stern, the junior house officer, and reported this to Kit, but they could make nothing of it.

Sue had been dreading Christmas. It was her first away from home and she had expected to be miserable. Everything she had ever heard or read, as well as her own imagination, told her that Christmas in a hospital must be, at best, a dreary business.

So she was surprised and cheered by the atmosphere of festivity which crept into the old corridors and animated the wards. Holly wreaths hung in every window. Huge Christmas trees appeared magically on the wards. The house officers were rehearsing an entertainment, nature unknown but the worst suspected, to be given in the rotunda before the entire staff, on Christmas Eve. A hundred professional singers would sing carols outside the hospital, also on Christmas Eve. A troupe of clowns and acrobats were to visit the Children's Ward Christmas afternoon — everybody invited. Everybody would have a special dinner, even the diabetics. Every patient would have a present from the hospital.

The patients, skeptical at first, and inclined to melancholy sighs, were carried out of themselves by the pervading excitement, and those who were able to be up and about found themselves perched on stepladders before the trees, their hands filled with tinsel and colored balls, and their ears ringing with instructions from the surrounding beds — instructions given often in the weakest of voices, but none the less urgent.

"Vait a minute — she's lopsided yet. A leetle higher — so!"

"No! No! *Madre di Dio!* Put-a da Christ child up top — way high!"

"Shure now — here's them blue lights ye like — I've put 'em where ye can see 'em."

In the evenings the Nurses' Homes rang with carols, for the Nurses' Glee Club, too, was practising, and would sing under all the ward windows at dawn on Christmas morning.

In the midst of all this preparation, Connie continued to be aloof and mysterious. Two days before Christmas she disappeared from her room for an entire evening, leaving the girls devoured with curiosity. She had been in uniform when she vanished, so she had not gone outside the hospital. She was not given to visiting in any rooms but those of her two friends, and she had not been called to the office for anything.

Sue and Kit waylaid her at the door of her room on her return.

"*Where've* you been?" they demanded. And Kit added suspiciously, "What's the idea of the canary whiskers?"

This phrase had been invented by Sue, and was used

by the three to describe a state of extreme satisfaction. Its origin was the old saying, "You look like the cat that's eaten the canary," and at the moment it fitted Connie's expression. Her face was bland, but the corners of her sensitive mouth curled upward and her hazel eyes held a look of utter contentment beneath their dark lashes.

She surveyed her two friends dreamily.

"I've been walking," she said.

Kit and Sue stared at her, open-mouthed.

"*Walking!* Where?"

"Oh, through the hospital." Connie's tone was airy.

"Through —" Kit turned to Sue. "She's been walking, through the *hospital* — it's such a treat for her."

"Yes," Sue said. "That would be it. And then, too, she gets so little exercise on the ward." She put an arm around Connie's shoulders and gazed at her tenderly. "Where does it hurt, dear? Tell Sue. Does your head ache? Spots before the eyes? Have you — er — heard voices when nobody was around — or is it just a dark shadow seen out of the tail of your eye, that vanishes when you look directly at it?"

Connie's grin was maddeningly complacent.

"Wouldn't you like to know!" she said and, ducking out from under Sue's arm, disappeared into her room, closing the door behind her.

"*Well —*" Kit said.

"We've been nourishing a viper, that's what we've been doing," Sue informed the closed door.

116

There was no answer.

The day before Christmas was unusually busy. There was no time for homesick musings, and, had there been, Sue was past indulging in them. Too many drawn white faces needed cheering; too many tired eyes waited hopefully to be made to twinkle.

Sue was late in coming off duty at the end of the day, and paused in her room only long enough to change to a fresh uniform before going over to the rotunda for the house officers' entertainment. Kit had left a note to say that she and Connie had gone on ahead, and would save a seat.

Sue snapped off her light and hurried to the elevator, glad to spare her aching feet the effort of carrying her down the stairs. Brewster House seemed completely emptied of nurses, and when Sue opened the door from the subway into the big brick corridor not a soul was visible. There was only an immense deserted space of bright lights. Sue quickened her steps, and then paused suddenly, halted by the sound of a familiar melody, faint but clear.

The city carol singers had come.

Double doors on the left of the corridor opened on the lawn. The shining brass knobs were icy under Sue's fingers as she stepped outside and closed the doors carefully behind her. She had forgotten the house officers' party.

For a moment, until her eyes became accustomed to the

darkness, she was conscious of nothing except the rhythm of the old hymn beating upward into the night from a hundred throats.

> "Silent night, Holy night,
> All is calm, all is bright,
> Round yon Virgin Mother and Child,
> Holy Infant so tender and mild . . ."

Sue's breath was a white cloud around her and her eyelids stung with the coldness of snowflakes clinging to them. She moved back into the shelter of the eaves and strained her eyes through the falling snow. At the far end of the lawn dark figures were massed beneath the windows of the oldest of the hospital's buildings. The thick walls stood in massive silence, the great dome brooding above them, and behind the long rows of dimly lighted windows Sue knew that aching heads lay motionless on their pillows, listening.

> "Sleep in heavenly peace,
> Sleep in heavenly peace!"

"If they only could," Sue thought.

Her eyes were tender, resting on the old walls. For more than a hundred years they had offered warmth and shelter to the sick. For a hundred years, beneath that dome, girls like herself, with aching feet and tired backs, had struggled side by side with young doctors to find better, surer ways to relieve pain.

AND THE GREATEST OF THESE

"Silent night, Holy night,
O, wondrous star, lend thy light . . ."

The door beside Sue opened abruptly. A white figure strode out into the darkness with a familiar, bounding walk, and stopped just beyond Sue, who stared thoughtfully at the proud head outlined against gray walls. The steadily descending snow blurred the stiff lines of Miss Cameron's uniform and softened the austerity of her features. The dim bulk of the hospital she had loved and served for so many years towered above her, as austere as herself.

"It's as though they were one spirit," Sue thought, looking from that compelling figure to the hospital beyond. "They take us in, all young and foolish, hundreds and hundreds of us through the years, and they send us out again with their brave mark upon us, and their strength behind us, always. Miss Waring was right. I'm beginning to understand."

The last words of the lovely old carol died away to a silence broken only by the soft hiss of the snow. Sue reached out for the doorknob, turned it gently, and slipped back into the warmth and light of the big brick corridor. Behind her, as she gave one last look back, she saw the motionless figure of Miss Cameron half hidden by swirling flakes. Sue's lips half formed the whispered words, "And the greatest of these is Love. . . ."

IX

CONNIE'S WAY

THE rotunda was brilliant with lights and murmurous with the sound of many voices speaking at once. Sue paused in one of the doorways to search the rows of faces for Kit and Connie. The majority of the audience was in uniform and the girls were difficult to distinguish in so much sameness. The only civilian clothes were worn by staff men and their wives, or an occasional nurse who had been having the afternoon off.

A five-piece orchestra was grouped in front and at the left, near the stairs leading up to the house officers' quarters. There was no stage, and no sign of a curtain for the play. The rotunda seemed quite as usual. Sue's eyes wandered over the audience until an arm in gray, with a white cuff, waved furiously from the fourth row, centre. There was no mistaking Kit's long fingers. Sue squeezed past knees and stepped on feet, the owners of which commented briskly and frankly upon her method of progress. She reached the empty seat at last, and sat down gratefully between Kit and Connie.

"Why did n't you pick a place that would be *really* hard to reach?" she demanded. "Don't you know that the ambition of my life is to step on as many feet as possible?"

"You're not so good at it, at that," Kit returned. "I distinctly saw three feet that you missed." She nudged Sue as she spoke, and glanced at Connie, whose only remark so far had been an absent-minded "Hello," after which she had lapsed into a state of lethargy.

"What's the matter with her now?" Sue whispered to Kit.

"I don't know. She's had the jitters all evening, and now she's practically unconscious. There's no use talking to her. Just ignore it."

Sue twisted in her seat to look over the audience once more.

"Golly," she said. "Everybody's here but the Egyptian mummies from the dome."

"Yes. Even Dr. Marston came. No — behind you, at the back. Miss Cameron's just sitting down by him."

Sue craned her neck, catching a momentary glimpse of Miss Cameron and of Dr. Marston's broad shoulders and pointed beard before a nurse sitting in front of him leaned forward to speak to someone and obscured her view.

Sue turned back to Kit.

"My! My!" she said. "I wish I'd worn my tiara! And, my dear, he was ruffling his beard up the wrong way again, even in this mob."

"Well, they do say, you know, that he even does it in his sleep. It's a sign of something, but I forget what."

"You would."

Kit's reply to this was not made, for at that moment a hush fell upon the audience as a short and chubby house officer, very newly arrived in the hospital, and occupying the position known as "pup," emerged through a door at the foot of the stairs, bearing a large placard which he displayed bashfully to the audience. The placard read: —

FIRST NUMBER
A BANJO SOLO BY
DR. PATRICK GLEASON

The audience applauded warmly and then became silent as the little house officer began to speak. His face was extremely red and his voice quavered.

"Ladies and gentlemen, we — er — we regret that there is no curtain — but — er — circumstances over which we have no control have made a curtain impossible. The — er — the lights will go out during changes of scene, and will the audience — er — please — er — not — I mean, will the audience — gosh! — please stay where you are!" he finished with a rush, and fled.

Dr. Gleason, very blond and self-possessed, came down the stairs armed with a banjo, seated himself on an operating-room stool near the piano, and played a brisk, if slightly discordant, tango, accompanied by the orchestra.

"I don't think he's so much," Kit commented under cover of the applause. "Can't they do better than this?"

Connie leaned forward and said sharply, "For goodness' sake, give them a chance! They've just begun!"
Kit stared at her, astonished.

Sue was reading the new placard displayed by the little house officer.

LESS THAN THE DUST

A SONG

DR. RONALD BENTON & CHORUS

A FAMOUS SURGEON — REPRESENTED BY

DR. WILLIAM BARRY

She turned suddenly upon Kit.

"Don't be so hasty," she said. "I'm sure it's going to be good."

The lights went out, leaving Kit in a martyred silence. The audience rustled and chattered in the darkness, waiting patiently for the lights, which came on at last, revealing Dr. Barry's tall, broad-shouldered figure standing at a little distance from the stairs.

His manner was haughty and forbidding. Over his uniform he wore the long white coat of visiting staff doctors, and his clean-cut features were disguised by a moustache and a pointed beard. When he raised a meditative hand and ruffled his beard the audience burst into a roar of laughter and with one accord turned to look back at Dr. Marston, who, though slightly red, was smiling broadly.

The orchestra swung into the opening bars of the song, and the audience, though unable to see any con-

nection between this and Dr. Marston, nevertheless settled back expectantly.

A rich tenor voice floated out over the audience from
the head of the stairs.

Young Dr. Benton was coming slowly down, his curling pale hair rippling over his head, his cherubic face
innocent and childlike, his eyes fixed upon Dr. Barry in
humble appeal. Behind him, two by two, came the
chorus of eight house officers, all in white.

The clear voice sang earnestly, tenderly: —

> "Less than the dust beneath thy rubber heel,
> Less than the rust that never stained thy Ford,
> Less than the trust thou hast in us, O lord,
> Even less than these — "

The last line was repeated solemnly by the chorus with
bowed heads, and the audience grinned, for the position
of the house officers in relation to the staff men was an
old joke. When the procession had reached Dr. Barry,
Dr. Benton knelt before him. The chorus formed a
semicircle behind, still bowed and humble.

> "Less than the weed we eat for spinach here,
> Less than the speed of hours spent far from thee,
> Less than the need thou hast in life of me,
> Even less are we."

At this point Dr. Benton prostrated himself, and Dr.
Barry, still in frozen silence, placed a large and substan-
tial foot upon his neck. The chorus knelt and bent their
foreheads to the floor, intoning: —

"Even less are we."

Dr. Benton's voice was necessarily somewhat muffled now, but his words were distinguishable.

> "Smile once, we pray, upon thy slaves, Great Chief,
> Say that some day we shall be mighty too,
> Say that we may be spared to be like you.
> Look down, O lord!"

"Look down, O lord," the chorus moaned as the lights went out.

The audience was not critical and the darkness was loud with applause. Starched aprons rustled, bibs crackled, and from all parts of the auditorium came the quick swish of shifting feet. A voice in the foreground suddenly remarked: —

"The audience will please refrain from acts of violence. Anyone wishing to escape may do so now. Line forms on the right. No scratching, please!"

The next offering was a sketch in which a tall house officer dressed in the white uniform and cap of a graduate nurse, and a small, fat house officer bulging in a probationer's uniform, gave an imitation of Miss Cameron teaching a probationer to make a bed, and ended with the collapse of the probationer, who was carried out on a stretcher. This was followed by a series of impersonations of important people in the hospital. No one's idiosyncrasies escaped, and there was a great deal of hilarity in the audience.

At the end of the impersonations the little house officer came out with his placard, which stated: —

FINALE

TO BE FOLLOWED BY DANCING

IN

THE ROTUNDA

There was a long pause in complete darkness. From the vicinity of the stairs thumpings were heard, accompanied by smothered masculine laughter and a curious scraping sound. Sue leaned back in her chair, too tired to make conversation. She could hear Kit's voice murmuring in the gloom to someone in the row behind. Connie, beside her, was motionless and silent.

At last, to everyone's surprise, a sudden cone of light shot out from high in the rear of the rotunda and focused on the floor near the stairs, revealing nothing whatever except a large wooden soapbox.

There was general laughter. Sue, peering into the darkness beyond the shaft of light, saw that a vague, dark form was moving slowly along the floor toward the box. The odd scraping sound continued. And then, suddenly, a face — a fantastic and incredible face — came into the spotlight over the edge of the soapbox. After her first shocked gulp Sue realized that she was looking at a gas mask. The pointed nose turned this way and that. The great glassy eyes were alive and watching. Long feelers waved from the forehead.

The figure clambered up onto the soapbox. The spotlight was full upon it, now, glittering on black folded wings nearly six feet long, which overlapped and tapered to a point. After a moment's pause the creature reared up stiffly until it stood upon black hind legs. Several pairs of middle legs were folded across its brown stomach. What these had been made from was uncertain, but the top pair, coming out from the shoulder, were covered with something suspiciously like black silk stockings, and ended in a pair of black mittens.

The likeness to a cockroach was unmistakable and the audience laughed, heartily at first, and then uncertainly, for the creature had a kind of dignity, and, strangely, a quality of wistfulness. The enormous round eyes above the peaked nose were turned appealingly on the audience. The feelers waved earnestly, and the top pair of arms — or legs — made little helpless movements, angular and futile.

"Jiminy!" someone whispered. "It's going to say something."

The thing cleared its throat, made a convulsive movement with its arms, and began to speak in a deep but hesitant baritone.

"Yes," it said. "You laugh at me. You despise me and my long line of descendants living here among you in lowliness and humility. No doubt you think of us as loathsome things, knowing only hunger and fear, worthy only of destruction."

The black mittens were clasped together in desperation. The round eyes appeared to grow larger.

"Do not despise us," it went on. "The hospital has not done so. We have our place. When we come out at night from the shelter of these old walls — when the little night winds whisk through the corridors and we play in the patches of moonlight on the floors — the hospital speaks to us in the darkness. The walls whisper to us as we scamper over them on tiny, silent feet."

The cockroach bent forward. Its voice was no longer hesitant.

"To *us,* the humblest, it is given to know the stories of forgotten years, held fast in the red brick and the granite. We hear the voice of tradition echoing through the corridors, as ponderous as the slow swing of stars above the dome. The little night winds, that were old when this hospital was young, tell us of the beginnings of the end of pain. They have watched the drama of medicine unfolding beneath this roof."

The deep voice had a sudden ring.

"The blue moonlight speaks to us in silver whispers, remembering the struggles, the failures, the triumphs, that have long since dropped into oblivion on the dust heap of the Past. These things — the moonlight — the winds — the stone — have seen you adding your little strength to the fight, giving your youth willingly for the honor of being part of it."

The ungainly figure straightened up. There was not a sound in the rotunda. The audience was held as one person by that vibrant voice.

"Your least effort here will never be lost. These old

walls do not forget. They are built upon your youth, your strength of purpose, your ideals. The sleepy moonlight knows it — and watches as you pass. The little night winds know, and touch your faces with cool fingers. We, too, know — so do not scorn us. We also belong, even as you belong. I thank you for your attention."

It bowed awkwardly and darkness blotted out the spotlight.

There was a moment of intense silence. Then walls and ceiling shook with the thunder of applause. The lights came up on an empty soapbox. The applause increased, and at length the cockroach returned, minus its original face, and clambered back on the box. The face it now wore was the face of Dr. William Barry.

He held up a black-mittened hand for silence.

"Ladies and gentlemen," he began, "I thank you again, and I would like to make an announcement. The house officers wish to extend public thanks to Miss Constance Halliday, who composed the cockroach's speech. She asked us not to reveal this, but we made no promises, and we feel — "

The rest was drowned in the uproar.

Sue whirled upon the crimson Connie and seized both her hands.

"You beast!" she cried. "Why did n't you tell us? Oh, Connie, I 'm all over gooseflesh!"

"Why — I — I — was it really — " Connie stammered. "I mean — "

People clapping her on the back and trying to shake

her hand made further speech impossible. Chairs and benches scraped and there was a general rustling as the audience rose and moved toward her.

"It was splendid, Miss Halliday, I can't tell you . . . Constance Halliday, how did you ever . . . That's the way I've always felt, but I never could — to think that you . . ."

Kit's eyes were warm with satisfaction as they rested on her friend.

"From now on," she announced, "I'm going to live on my reputation as Connie's pal — the girl who knows a hospital when she sees one!"

The nurses around them fell back suddenly to make way for Miss Matthews, and behind her — Miss Cameron.

"It was very nice indeed, Miss Halliday. I'm glad to know that you have so much feeling for the hospital. You must write something for the school magazine."

Connie's flush deepened painfully, but before she could speak Miss Cameron pressed forward, grim as always, but with smiling eyes.

"That was splendid, Miss Halliday. I'm proud of you."

Sue felt a hand close on her arm and turned to meet the eyes of Ward 7's dish nurse.

"I take it all back," the latter said earnestly. "You were right. She's more than O.K. I'm for her!" And she added in a lower tone, "So is everybody else. We had no idea she felt like that."

Sue grinned. The nurses were closing in on Connie

again, and she was looking around her desperately for some avenue of escape.

"Wait a minute, everybody," Sue cried. "Miss Halliday has no statement to make at this time. Flowers may be delivered to her manager. Miss Halliday's nervous system must not be subjected to any strain. Please make way!"

She guided Connie through the laughing crowd, and their progress was marked by a ripple of applause. As they approached the door Connie's steps quickened. In the hall outside Sue halted.

"Don't go," she pleaded. "Be a good egg and stay for the dance."

Connie shook her head.

"Everybody's being so nice — I'm afraid I'd break down — or something." Her eyes twinkled at Sue through wet lashes. "Think of my nervous system!" She turned to go, but Sue caught her hand.

"Connie," she said, "everything's awfully all right, now, isn't it?"

"Yes. Everything's more all right than it's ever been in my life before."

Sue nodded.

"I'm awfully glad. And Connie — "

"What?"

"Merry Christmas!"

X

TROUBLE

THE excitement of wearing a gray uniform and of being a regular nurse was gradually subsiding.

Immediately after the New Year, classes began again, and Sue discovered that probation, though a nervous strain, was easy compared to working eight hours a day on the ward, with classes in the evening and in one's off-duty time.

The lectures on medical and surgical work were called clinics. The class was taken around the wards to see those patients whose illnesses were the subjects of the lectures. Sue was surprised to find that the patients enjoyed this. Each felt himself or herself to be a "very unusual case" and consequently important — not realizing that the typicalness of the case was what made it interesting.

There were lectures on dietetics, lectures on the properties of medicines, lectures on embryology — which meant studying the growth of a living baby from its first cellular form to the moment of its birth. Bandage class was held three evenings a week in the basement of Grafton Hall. This was a very informal class, and the nurses ran about talking and laughing while they bandaged each other, literally from head to foot, under the amused eye of the instructor.

On the first of February Sue was transferred back to the Women's Surgical side, to Ward 27, and was told that she would have a period of relief duty and then begin night work.

Relief duty meant having from eleven o'clock until three off duty, and then remaining on the ward until eleven o'clock at night, when the night nurse came on. In this way Sue would acquire a little experience before going on regular night duty. It seemed to her a great deal of experience, and she felt fully prepared for her month of night work until the very last moment. Then panic seized her.

The afternoon before she went on night duty was spent in remembering all the stories she had ever heard about the things that happen in a hospital at night — nurses falling asleep and being expelled — patients suddenly going insane, or having heart attacks, or trying to escape from the hospital. And she had been told over and over again that a night nurse was responsible for everything that happened on her ward while she was on duty.

She was in a state of numb terror when she set out for the ward at last, hearing as from a great distance the echoing of her footsteps in the deep well of the stairs leading to Ward 27. She was sure something was following her, and once, just before she reached the second landing, she looked over her shoulder in spite of herself, but there was nothing there. On the threshold of Ward 27 she paused. Once she had stepped over it she would be a night nurse.

For a moment there seemed no ward there — only great dark shadows creeping toward a pool of light on the head nurse's desk. The relief nurse was sitting before it folding gauze sponges, the light yellow on her swiftly moving hands. The huge square chimney in the centre of the ward by the desk had now but a single side, faintly white. The rest was in darkness. And then far back in the shadows dim rows of beds took shape. The ward smelled fresh and cool, and there was no sound except the sound of breathing. It must have been the same last night, Sue thought, when she, herself, was the relief nurse. But she had n't noticed it then.

She stepped over the threshold and the relief nurse looked up.

"Oh, hello," she said, as Sue loomed beside her. "Everything 's peaceful. You 'll have an easy night. Pull up a chair and I 'll give you the night orders."

Sue brought a chair from beside one of the beds and sat down. The rustling of her apron was unnaturally loud in the stillness.

"Now," the relief nurse began, "Mrs. Wolf — appendix — can have a sixth of morphia every three hours if she needs it — but she won't. She 's had one already, and that 'll hold her. But watch her for staining.

"Miss Parsons — varicose veins — no orders — she 's all right — sleeps all night — "

The voice droned on as the relief nurse turned the pages of the order book. When she had finished, she rose, glancing at her watch.

"I 'd better be getting out of here. I 've blocked out your night report — look." She handed Sue the small pasteboard-covered book. "I 've filled in the names and diagnoses for you, and marked the places for the seven, eleven, and three o'clock temperatures."

"Thanks awfully."

Sue walked to the door with her, and stood listening to the sound of her receding footsteps with an empty feeling in the pit of her stomach. Then she went back into the ward and slowly made the rounds of the beds. No one moved or spoke. On relief duty the patients had been wakeful and talkative and the ward had been pleasantly alive. Now there was only the rustling of her apron to fill the shadows with noise. She noticed for the first time that her shoes made a squishing sound on the linoleum with every step.

The long night stretched before her, silent and lonely.

Sue paused only a moment in the deserted whiteness of the kitchen. The linen closet was better. It was neat and still, but the light glowed warmly on the folded red of bathrobes and the yellow of blankets. Her shoes squished again in the passageway, and then the laboratory was grinning at her with rows of shining bottles.

The thought of Mrs. Wolf came to her suddenly and she hurried back to the cool dimness of the ward, to raise the bedclothes and turn her flashlight on the dressing. It was white and smooth. There was no red stain. Mrs. Wolf sighed and burrowed deeper into her pillow.

At midnight the nurse in the adjoining ward came in to relieve Sue for lunch, and assured her that there would be house officers and supervisors around all night. Sue had known this, but hearing someone say it again made it seem more real. And after the lively conversation of the nurses in the dining room, the ward, when Sue returned to it, seemed less isolated.

She settled down at the desk to read over the book of instructions for night nurses. The rules were brief and to the point: —

Temperature of the ward shall not exceed 68 degrees.

In any emergency notify the night supervisor before calling the house officer.

The ward must be in order before the nurse goes off duty, laundry bags marked, dishes collected, etc.

The night report must be ready for the supervisor by 6 A. M.

Turn on steam table in kitchen at 5 A. M.

Start toast at 6 A. M.

Sue read on, down the list. Then she opened the night report and began to jot down a few notes. Just when the pen became unmanageable she did not know. She only knew that it was suddenly both heavy and loose in her hand, and it made, quite by itself, strange little wavering marks on the page. Her eyes burned, and the lids were pulled down by enormous weights.

She tried to look at what she had written, but when she

held the page away from her and stared with wide-open eyes, the lines blurred before them, and when she held the book close and squinted her eyes closed.

Sue laid down the pen. At least, she meant to lay it down, but she had a confused feeling that actually it had jumped out of her hand. There could n't be any harm in resting her eyes for an instant by closing them. Perhaps they would stop burning. Her lids dropped gratefully, and what had been her body, sitting on a chair, with its elbows on a desk, became a formless void.

Her cheek struck the blotter with a smack.

Sue struggled to her feet. Far in the back of her mind a tiny voice was saying, "This won't do — this won't do — this won't do."

She would go out in the kitchen, she thought dully, and splash her face with cold water. She turned, stupefied with sleep — and found herself face to face with the night supervisor.

Sue's mind came awake with a shocking jerk. How long had Miss Ellison been standing there?

The supervisor waited, motionless, a slender, smart figure with dark hair and shrewd brown eyes. At last she said: —

"Good evening, Miss Barton."

"Good evening, Miss Ellison."

"Miss Barton, when you feel like that I would advise you to walk about the ward a little."

"Yes, Miss Ellison."

"Is everything all right here?"

"Yes, Miss Ellison."

"What was Mrs. Wolf's eleven-o'clock temperature?"

"I —" Sue faltered. She had forgotten the eleven-o'clock temperatures in the excitement of coming on night duty for the first time — and forgetfulness was the unpardonable sin. Frantic thoughts scurried through her mind in meaningless confusion. Then one stood out suddenly, by itself. "Never wake a patient." Sue straightened up and said with absolute truth, "Mrs. Wolf has been asleep ever since I came on, Miss Ellison."

The supervisor's eyes were piercing.

"I see," she said. "Are you watching her for staining?"

"Yes, Miss Ellison."

"When did you look at her last?"

"Just a few minutes ago."

"Very well."

The supervisor's eyes were cold as she turned and moved toward the beds, looking carefully at each patient as she passed. Sue followed close behind. When the inspection was done and the white figure of the supervisor had rustled into the next ward, Sue fled to the kitchen, but there was no longer any necessity for splashing cold water on her face. She was thoroughly awake.

"I'm in wrong at the very beginning," she thought, pacing back and forth in the narrow white space. Miss Ellison had caught her almost asleep, but that might be passed over because this was her first night. If only she had n't faltered when Miss Ellison asked about that temperature!

"She *knew* I'd forgotten," Sue whispered to the steam table. "She knew, and she'll remember it — and if anything else happens — "

The thought pursued her all night. Even the rush of the early morning work could not quite obliterate it. On her way off duty at seven, Sue met Miss Waring in the downstairs corridor and the repose in Miss Waring's young face moved her to blurt out the whole story. If Miss Waring thought everything was really all right, it would be all right.

But to Sue's dismay Miss Waring seemed troubled.

"Mercy, child!" she said when Sue had finished and stood waiting, her cap askew on tumbled red curls. "It's a pity this had to happen on your first night. Miss Ellison will be watching you from now on. But don't worry," she added, seeing the terror in Sue's eyes. "It's not as bad as all that. Very likely nothing else will happen in your whole night duty, and you'll come off with Miss Ellison thinking you the best night nurse she's ever had. Make her think that. You can, you know."

"I'll try," Sue promised gratefully. And for a time it seemed that nothing else would happen, but her confidence in herself was shaken. She no longer dared to sit down at the desk after midnight for fear that the treacherous sleepiness would steal upon her, and she spent long hours wandering about the ward, looking at the sleeping patients in an agony of envy.

She marveled that they did n't lie awake for the sheer pleasure of feeling the smoothness of sheets over them —

the warmth of blankets — the softness of pillows under their cheeks. There they lay, relaxed, inert, engulfed in a warm tide of sleep. Over in Brewster Kit and Connie slept too, night after night, untroubled, sure of themselves, while Sue worked always with the feeling that things were getting away from her somehow. She went to see Miss Waring again, and came away somewhat irritated, for Miss Waring, to Sue's surprise, had said crisply: —

"If you feel that way, my dear, then you are not doing your best. There is no reason why the work should get away from you. You have ability and the work is not difficult, really. The other nurses can do it, and so can you. You'll have to buckle down to it."

Sue felt that this judgment was most unfair. She *was* doing her best. And even Miss Waring was failing her.

The very next night Miss Ellison found a heap of soiled laundry on the floor of the laboratory and spoke to Sue about it rather sharply. Two nights later, following up a strange odor, the supervisor discovered a pair of rubber gloves burned to a crisp in the sterilizer.

Sue assured herself that these things were not unusual. They happened all over the hospital. The whole trouble lay in the fact that Miss Ellison was down on her.

At the beginning of her third week of night duty Sue came on the ward one night to find three ether patients and five new admissions. There would be no time for making sponges, and she was already behind with them. Well, she would show Miss Ellison this time.

That night the house officer, anxious about the ether

patients, made several visits to the ward. He was a pleasant boy, with sandy hair and an earnest, freckled face. She liked him, for he had more than once gone out of his way to explain to her about a case, or to help her with a heavy patient. On his last visit, toward three in the morning, he found Sue halfway up the linen-closet shelves in search of an extra warm blanket.

She heard his step and looked down, smiling. The linen-closet light glared full upon him and she saw that his face was white with exhaustion.

"You 'd better go to bed," she remarked briskly from her perch. "You look all in."

"I will — and I am. I 'm going right now. But I wanted to tell you that I 've changed the order on that laporotomy. You 'd better give her a quarter of morphine instead of a sixth — and if she does n't sleep please call me."

"Of course." Sue dropped to the floor, the blanket in her arms. "But I think I can get her comfortable enough so that she 'll sleep without my having to drag you out again."

"I 'm sure you can." He glanced at her in some concern. "You look a bit tired, yourself," he offered. Then he grinned. "What you ought to have to-night is a pair of roller skates."

Sue considered this.

"Ye-yes," she said. "But don't you think a scooter would be more practical? Roller skates don't seem to care for me."

They both laughed — and then Sue's heart contracted and her breath stopped.

Miss Ellison was standing in the door of the linen closet. "Good morning, Dr. Lake," she said. Then, to Sue, "I'd like to speak to you for a moment, Miss Barton."

Dr. Lake's white uniform melted into the gloom. Still clutching the blanket, Sue followed Miss Ellison out to the desk and there the supervisor turned to face her.

Sue clasped the blanket more tightly against the pounding of her heart, and waited for the end.

Miss Ellison's eyes were very black.

"I'd like to see you paying a little attention to the patients, Miss Barton," she said in tones of ice. "I will not have them neglected. You have a heavy ward to-night, and it is not a time to be chatting in the linen closet with house officers."

"But I wasn't chatting, Miss Ellison," Sue began desperately. "Dr. Lake came to — "

"That will do. I heard part of the conversation. It was enough." The supervisor hesitated, for Sue's face was white with misery. "I realize," she went on more gently, "that this is your first night duty, and that you are very young. I believe that your intentions are good, but you have a great deal to learn. I hope," she finished, "that you will try to do better, and that I shall not have to speak to you again about this."

"Yes, Miss Ellison."

Sue felt trapped and helpless. Why, now, when she was making a real effort, should everything go wrong? What was the use in trying? Always before she had done things well without any effort, and now she could n't seem to do anything.

Sue was too young to know that all her trouble arose from the fact that she had never had to make an effort. She wanted to do well, but things had come too easily to her, and the determination so necessary now was still dormant. She thought that she was trying, but her determination expended itself in merely wishing.

On her very last night of night duty, about midnight, she was doing a dressing when a little hand bell at the far end of the ward rang softly.

"Somewan 's afther wantin' ye, dearie," said her patient.

"It 's Mrs. Harper, way over in the corner," Sue said, reaching for another sponge. "I can't think what she 'd want. I had her all settled for the night. Anyway, she 's able to be up and about, and I can't leave you like this." Her fingers flew.

When the last safety pin was in place in the fresh dressing, Sue rearranged the pillows to ease the pull on sore muscles, and straightened up to go to Mrs. Harper, when the telephone rang, a scream of command in the stillness of the ward.

Ward telephones must not be allowed to go on ringing. Sue hurried to answer it.

"Ward 27. Miss Barton speaking."

"Hello, Sue," came the hearty voice of Grace Holton, on duty in the Emergency Ward. "We 're sending you an accident case right away — fractured skull — patient 's unconscious — they 're on the way up to you now."

"Oh, don't mind me," Sue replied. "I have n't a thing to do!"

Mrs. Harper's bell tinkled again as Sue hung up the receiver and hurried to the linen closet for blankets. Mrs. Harper would have to wait a few minutes. There was not a moment to lose if the accident case was on the way up. Sue's mind shut down in sudden concentration on the things needed for the new patient.

She was frantically remaking an empty bed when Mrs. Harper rang again, more loudly this time. It was incredible that a tiny bell could make so much noise. It would wake patients who could sleep through the sound of foot steps or voices. Everybody would wake up and want things. It would take an hour to get the ward quiet again — and with an accident case coming which would need all her attention! Maybe when Mrs. Harper saw the accident case coming — but no, she could n't see. The chimney was in the way. Well . . .

Sue hurried, tucking in the heavy blankets, placing hot water bags. Mrs. Harper rang again.

The bed was ready. Now for Mrs. Harper.

The telephone screamed.

Sue rushed to it and said pleasantly that the patient Smith was having a comfortable night. "Or was," she thought grimly, and turned to go at last to Mrs. Harper. She had taken but one step when she saw, coming through the door at the end of the ward, the accident case, on a stretcher, and accompanied by a nurse, two orderlies, and Dr. Lake. They lifted the patient to the bed and hurried out, Dr. Lake pausing only long enough to write the orders for the new admission.

Sue tucked the heated blankets about the motionless figure of the accident case, and tried to settle the bandaged head more comfortably.

"The poor thing!" she thought, suddenly conscious of her own strong young body. Only a little while ago this woman, too, had been well and strong, never dreaming what was to happen to her. Drat Mrs. Harper! For Mrs. Harper was ringing again, and this time she continued to ring without stopping.

Sue reached the bedside at last, and the ringing stopped.

"I 'm so sorry, Mrs. Harper," she said. "I could n't come before. There was an emergency case on the way up. What can I do for you?"

Mrs. Harper was sitting up in bed, the bell in her hand. She stared at Sue in icy disbelief.

"I 'd like to have that window lowered two inches. There 's a draught blowing on the bed — and I want to tell you right now, Miss Barton, that I 'm going to report you for this. The idea of keeping a sick person waiting!"

Sue lowered the window two inches. "I 'm very sorry, Mrs. Harper," she said briefly. "I could n't come before."

"You need n't make excuses! I shall — "

"What seems to be the trouble?"

It was Miss Ellison's voice.

Sue turned to face the white figure standing in the shadows behind her, and opened her mouth to speak, but Mrs. Harper was ahead of her. She pointed a shaking finger at Sue and said harshly: —

"I want to report this nurse. She don't do her work! I rang for her twenty minutes before she came. I won't stand for it!"

Mrs. Ellison's face was impassive.

"I 'm sure Miss Barton did n't mean to neglect you," she said soothingly. "Our nurses don't do that sort of thing."

Sue spoke quickly. "It was the accident case, Miss Ellison — "

"I don't believe there was an accident case!" Mrs. Harper snapped.

"Indeed there was," Miss Ellison assured her. "I have just come up myself to see about it. I know that Miss Barton came as quickly as she could."

Sue's relief was short-lived. At the desk Miss Ellison confronted her with furious eyes.

"*What* is the meaning of this disgraceful scene, Miss Barton?"

Sue explained.

The supervisor's face cleared somewhat as she listened.

"I 'm sorry this happened, Miss Barton," she said when Sue had finished. "It was not your fault, of course, though I think that if you had tried you could have found a moment in which to speak to this patient and explain to her, before she had time to become so angry. I believe that you did what you thought was right, but you showed poor judgment. It is on a par with the rest of your night work. I'm sorry to have to tell you this, Miss Barton, but your night work has been far from satisfactory. Miss Matthews is disappointed in you."

"But I wasn't able — "

"A good nurse, Miss Barton, is always able to do a little more than she can."

It was with these words ringing in her ears that Sue finished her last night of night duty. She had failed. Even Miss Matthews knew it.

She slept fitfully that day, and woke in the middle of the afternoon feeling as though her chest were being crushed under a heavy weight. It was several minutes before she remembered the reason for it.

"I might as well go out and get some fresh air," she thought.

But the gayety of the winter streets did not lift her mood. She had no idea where she was walking, and no sense of surprise when a voice behind her said: —

"Well! If it isn't Miss Barton!"

Sue turned listlessly.

"Good afternoon, Dr. Barry."

He looked very tall and very nice in street clothes, and he was beaming. She mustn't let him know. She couldn't bear to let him know. He thought she was a good nurse. Sue pulled herself together and managed a smile.

He glanced at her colorless face in surprise.

"See here," he said, "you look frozen to death. You ought — " He hesitated, and then said impulsively:

147

"What you need is something hot. There's a tea room just down the street. Won't you have tea with me?"

Sue assented gratefully. Here was a friend, someone who believed in her, and whose buoyant spirits might lift her out of this strange cold misery. Beyond that, she did not think at all.

As they moved on together down the street the pale gold of the winter sun was caught in Sue's curls, and Dr. Barry's eyes were very blue as he looked down at her. Sue did n't notice. She was thinking that the tea room looked very inviting. Dr. Barry pushed open the door, and they went in.

Neither of them saw the round face and startled eyes of Miss Mason, the assistant superintendent of nurses, looking at them from the window of a passing trolley car.

Dr. Barry was very entertaining and Sue's natural good spirits began to assert themselves. She was almost herself again when Dr. Barry put her into a taxi and gave the driver the address of the hospital.

"I have shopping to do," he explained. "Ties and things."

Sue laughed and the taxi bumped away over the icy streets. Things were n't so bad after all — perhaps. She was still smiling when she ran up the steps of Brewster and paused to look at the mail on the hall table. Her eye fell on a square white envelope addressed to herself. It had no postmark and no stamp. Her name was written upon it, but nothing else.

Sue opened it, wondering, and then the color drained

from her face, leaving it chalky white. The note inside read: —

Miss Barton:
   You will report to Miss Matthews in her office at six P. M.

XI

"A GOOD TIME WAS HAD BY ALL"

KIT and Connie were already at their favorite table when Sue came into the dining room at six-thirty. Neither of them noticed that she was unusually quiet, because they were engaged in a heated discussion with Lois Wilmont. A discussion with Lois required all of anyone's attention, both for purposes of argument and for keeping one's temper.

Sue did n't join in the discussion. She was very pale, and her fingers, playing with a spoon, shook a little as she sat listening.

"If you are n't willing to make sacrifices," Lois was saying, "you should n't be a nurse."

"I was n't talking about willingness," Kit said. "I simply asked *why?* It's all very well for Miss Pickering to rant around in ethics class about the-patient-must-be-saved-at-all-costs tradition. Nursing is a profession, just like the law or any other. If a man is consulting a lawyer and suddenly goes mad in the office, there's no tradition which says the lawyer can't run out of the room and call the police. He does n't have to stay and get a black eye trying to keep his client from jumping out of the window, or what not."

"There is n't any tradition," Lois said hotly, "but there ought to be. We all owe a duty to humanity."

"Good old humanity," Kit said, grinning.

Hilda Grayson spoke before Lois could launch forth on humanity.

"But," she offered humbly, "the man is paying the lawyer for advice, is n't he? He pays the nurse to keep him from jumping out the window when he 's nuts. Is n't that the difference?"

"Of course it is," Grace Holton cried. "That 's the stuff, Hilda."

Lois regarded Hilda with scorn.

"Money has nothing to do with it," she said. "Nurses have chosen to give up their lives to keeping people in good health, mentally and physically. That 's all there is to it."

Kit's brown eyes began to sparkle with exasperation.

"Honestly, Willie," she said, "your principles are a positive menace. If somebody does n't kill you first you 're going to have more darn fun starving to death. Of course you 'll work for nothing when you graduate?"

Lois did not flush. "I —" she began.

"Wait a minute," Connie interposed quietly. "We 're getting off the subject. The original question was whether we 'd have the courage to risk our lives for a patient in an emergency."

Lois straightened up in her chair.

"Certainly I 'd have the courage. Don't be ridiculous!"

"How do you know you would? Have you ever —"

"But look, Connie." Kit's voice was very British. "It

151

does n't matter whether you 'd dare or not. It 's one of those things you simply do — at least I hope so," she added hastily.

Connie glanced across the table at Sue.

"What do you think, Bat?" she asked.

Sue blinked.

"I — what?"

"For heaven's sake," Kit moaned. "Do you mean to say you 've been sitting here in the middle of a world-shaking discussion and have n't been listening?"

Sue dropped her spoon. Her soup was untouched.

"Why, I — why, no, I 'm afraid I have n't."

Hilda was looking at her intently.

"What 's the matter with you, Sue?" she said. "You look sort of green. Don't you feel well?"

Sue stirred uneasily. Then she said, with a gayety she was far from feeling: —

"Oh, I 'm as well as could be expected, considering that I 've been romping around the T.S.O. — with Miss Matthews. I don't know how she came out of it, but I feel like a well-cooked sponge."

"*What!*"

Even Lois raised her voice to join in the shriek.

"The T.S.O.! What *for?*"

Sue looked at the startled faces. They 'd be more startled in a minute.

"Well — for this and that, and having tea with a house officer."

There was a stunned silence. Grace Holton was the first to recover.

"Yoicks!" she cried. "Did they expel you?"

"No, not quite. But I had a couple of bad moments."

"Really, Sue," said Lois Wilmont, "I never would have believed you were the kind of girl to do a thing like that. I'm disappointed in you."

Sue flushed.

"I'm sorry to have shattered your ideals, Willie. You'll just have to grow another crop."

"What happened, Sue?" Kit asked. "Maybe hearing all the dirt will mend Willie's broken heart."

"Well, you see, Miss Ellison is down on me. I guess she reported me in the first place. And then with this business about the tea, Miss Matthews decided that I was deteriorating — no sense of responsibility — me, who am second only to Willie in earnestness!"

Sue paused. Her pose of indifference was hard to maintain when she remembered the cutting tones of Miss Matthews's voice. A faint smell of furniture polish somewhere in the dining room brought back the smell of Miss Matthews's office, and her heart began to pound again. But the interview was all over. She mustn't let it get her like this. Connie's quiet voice reached her like a steadying hand. Connie was not deceived.

"Go on, Sue."

"Yes, do go on, Barton," Willie put in eagerly.

"Well, she was rather decent about it. She believed me

153

when I said that meeting the house officer was an accident. She even believed me when I said that I did n't think about the hospital rule when I had tea with him. It was the truth," she finished simply.

None of the girls asked the name of the house officer, and Sue was grateful, for she knew they were curious. But there was no point in dragging Dr. Barry into a tangle of hospital gossip. She went on more briskly: —

"I promised her I 'd be good and eat my spinach. And she said that was all she asked — for me to try. The final decision was that I was to try — a decision reached, I may say, at the cost of my entire nervous system."

"I think," said the undaunted Lois, "that you 're being extremely flippant about a very serious matter. You don't seem to realize — "

Connie interrupted her.

"Why don't we take your nervous system out and amuse it? There's a frightfully good movie on at the Metropolitan. Let's go."

"All right. I 'd love to — oh, my goodness, I forgot! That's one of the things — no late passes for me for a month. It was the last thing Miss Matthews said."

"Oh, don't worry, Sue," Kit said. "If we go the minute Connie and I are off duty we can be back by ten. You won't need a late pass."

Connie's wisdom in suggesting a movie proved sound. Sue had expected to be unable to keep her mind on the picture, but before she had been half an hour in the theatre she had forgotten her own difficulties in her absorption in those of the screen heroine. It was an unusually long picture, and Kit glanced at her watch as they came out of the theatre.

"Girls!" she gasped. "It's ten minutes to ten! We'll have to run like mad! If Sue's late to-night she'll be in an awful jam. Come on!"

"Grab a taxi," Connie cried.

They scrambled into the first cab that appeared, begging the driver to hurry. He was sympathetic, and the taxi rocked and skidded over the icy streets in his attempt to satisfy his almost hysterical fares. When they reached the long hill above the hospital he slowed down.

"It ain't no use," he said through the window. "I gotta go easy here, or we'll have a bust-up."

Sue's nails cut into her palm, as the taxi crept down the slope, inch by inch. At last she could stand it no longer.

"Let's get out and run, kids," she begged. "We can fall down this hill faster than he's going. What time is it?"

"It's one minute to ten," Kit wailed. "Oh, Sue, I'm so sorry!"

It was eight minutes after ten when they raced up the steps of Brewster. The windows were dark and only a dim light burned in the hall. They tried the door stealthily. It was locked. They had known that it would be locked.

"Which maid is on duty?" Connie whispered. "If it's Norah she might let us in and not say anything about it."

The maid's office was across the hall from the door. The girls ran around the end of the wing and looked through the window. Norah was not there. In her place sat Mrs. Fitch, an elderly maid known as "Pug." She was engrossed in a copy of *True Confessions,* mouthing the words as she read.

"She looks like a caterpillar eating a leaf," Kit murmured.

"Ssssh!" Connie dragged Kit out of range of the light from the window. "Oh, why couldn't it have been Norah? Pug reports everything!"

For a moment Sue felt actually sick. The necessity for doing something about their situation saved her. As always in an emergency, the girls turned to her.

"Listen," Sue whispered. "If there were any way to get in a window one of us could climb in and unlock the side door for the other two. Pug never goes near the side door."

They tiptoed along the walk, yearning at the windows and trying to keep the hard-packed snow from squeaking beneath their feet. There was no hope of arousing any of their friends. It was probable that none of them were asleep yet, but all their class had rooms on the third and fourth floors. The first floor was given over to the living room and the infirmary. The second floor was their only chance, and they weren't sure which nurses occupied the second-floor rooms.

Sue was certain of but one thing — somehow she was going to get into Brewster without being reported. She *must!*

"The ivy!" she whispered suddenly.

Without another word the three rushed over to the wall of the building and felt along it among the vines for one thick enough to bear a heavy weight. They found one at last. It was as thick as Sue's arm, and went up between the windows for fully three stories, as nearly as they could see in the starlight. The windows on both sides of it were open, for the girls could see the curtains blowing out, faintly white in the darkness.

"Do hurry!" Kit hissed. "I'm freezing. Who's going to be the trapeze performer?"

Sue had already considered this.

"I will," she said. "You're too heavy, Kit, and Connie's skirt is too tight."

"Which window?" Connie breathed.

Sue peered up at the dark wall.

"The one on the right. It's nearest the vine."

"Whose is it? You'd better be careful, Sue!"

"How should I know whose it is?" Sue pulled on her gloves and took a firm grip on the rough vine. "Anyway, whoever's in there is going to get a surprise in a minute."

Connie had been examining the vine.

"Oh, Sue, wait a minute — it — it looks dangerous! Why not throw a snowball and wake up whoever is there?"

"And stir up the whole house smacking snowballs against the wall? Not a chance!"

157

"Well, you'd better say something to her before you go in," Kit suggested. "You don't want her screeching her head off."

"Good idea. I will."

The vine shook under Sue's weight. She clung to it desperately, feeling her way and trying to keep the toes of her shoes from scraping on the bricks. Some of the smaller vines began to tear away from the wall, but the main vine held.

The rows of bricks moved jerkily downward past her face until the first-story windows were below her. Just a little farther and she would be safe on the ledge of that open window. She was panting now. It was a long time since she had done any climbing. The vine was getting smaller, frailer.

The shadowy window sill was on a level with her shoulders.

"There goes my stocking," she thought.

She reached out and grasped the window ledge beside her with one hand. Her right knee struck the corner of the ledge sharply, and her eyes filled with tears of pain and exasperation. Inch by inch she wormed her way onto the ledge, still clinging to the ivy with one hand.

She was safe! She'd done it!

The window yawned black before her and the curtain, blowing across her face, blinded her for an instant. The steam-heated air of the room was a wall of warmth. Sue fought with the folds of the curtain. There!

She peered into the room.

"Sssst!" she said.

There was no answer.

She scrambled into the room, fell over a chair, and bent to look closely at the bed. It was empty. Sue could have cheered.

She moved to the door and looked cautiously into the corridor — to see, coming briskly toward her, the bath-robed figure of Miss Aden, youngest and newest of the supervisors in the Training School Office. She was carrying a towel and soap.

Sue went under the bed in one leap.

Miss Aden's steps came nearer and paused at the door of the room in which Sue was hidden. A hand fumbled for the switch and the light blazed on, the door closed, and a pair of white shoes went past Sue's nose, over the little rug.

The only reason that Sue didn't faint was because she never had and didn't know how. She lay motionless against the wall, scarcely breathing, while the white shoes came and went at the foot of the bed. She listened, almost in a stupor, to the rustle of garments being removed. The white shoes swooped upward, one after the other, and dropped to the floor again, empty. A hand reached down and turned off the radiator.

There was a pause. Then the light clicked off, and over Sue's head the mattress and bedsprings sagged down, creaking.

Sue's thoughts cleared with the return of darkness, and presented her with a picture of Kit and Connie slowly freezing to death. When Miss Aden was asleep — but if she were a light sleeper she would certainly be wakened by any attempt Sue might make to get out of the room. If she were a heavy sleeper there was a chance. Sue remembered, suddenly, that Miss Aden was noted for her timidity and nervousness. Nervous people were nearly always light sleepers.

Sue moaned inwardly.

Somewhere in the room the ticking of a clock became audible. The sound seemed to grow louder as time passed. A slit of yellow light appeared on the floor and widened very slowly.

The moon was up.

Sue was aching with cold, but nothing would have induced her to move hand or foot. She watched the moonlight with dull eyes. It was almost a square on the floor now. And still Miss Aden tossed and turned. Sue wondered in a sudden panic if the supervisor felt that she was not alone in the room. People did have those feelings sometimes.

In the increased light Sue could see the lower part of the room quite clearly. The white shoes stood mutely side by side on the rug in front of the little rocking-chair. One of the rockers was on the edge of the rug — on the edge — the rocker . . .

Sue held back her gasp with an effort.

Miss Aden turned over again. Sue looked up at the

mattress. It was a thin mattress and the outline of Miss Aden's body was distinct. She was facing the room, lying on her side.

Sue's hand was steady as she reached out and took hold of the corner of the rug — moved it a little. The rocking-chair began to rock. Sue moved the rug more vigorously. The chair leapt forward several inches.

There was a scrambling over Sue's head, and a choking sound.

Sue pulled at the rug again, and the chair nodded back and forth in the moonlight.

There was an ear-splitting shriek. The supervisor's bare feet struck the floor, bounded once. The door jerked open, and the sound of screams and running feet grew faint in the distance.

Sue was a dark fleeing shadow down the corridor in the opposite direction. Doors were opening behind her. There were voices. Miss Aden was still screaming somewhere in the vicinity of the elevator.

Sue did n't stop until she had reached the first floor and the side door.

She unlocked it and Kit and Connie fell into her arms, stiff with cold and scarcely able to walk.

"I said you 'd come," Connie whispered. "I knew you would."

"What happened?" Kit demanded.

Sue told them briefly, and they grinned in speechless delight.

It was an hour before Brewster was quiet again and the

girls dared to leave the darkness of the side-door entrance and creep upstairs to their rooms.

"Good night," Sue whispered from her doorway. "And thank you so much for a pleasant evening."

"Don't mention it," Kit returned. "A good time was had by all."

XII

NELLIE

FOR several days the hospital buzzed with accounts of Miss Aden's extraordinary behavior. The house officers were of the opinion that she had had an optical illusion. The nurses decided that it was only a nightmare. Miss Aden denied both assertions with violence. She had not been asleep, she insisted, and furthermore she had not only seen the chair rocking all by itself in the moonlight, but she had *heard* it. The sound was what had first drawn her attention to it.

Kit, Connie, and Sue wondered loudly with the rest, and Kit made a very capable speech to a group of nurses in the living room of Brewster, upholding the optical-illusion theory, and proving that Miss Aden could very well have had an auditory hallucination in the beginning which would have acted suggestively upon the optic nerve.

The excitement died down after a time, and was superseded by the juniors' minstrel show. Sue went on duty in the Out-Patient Department, and was so busy and interested that the memory of her escapade seemed half a dream — something that had happened to somebody else.

The memory of her interview with Miss Matthews, however, remained vivid. The matter of the tea did n't worry

Sue very much. Incredibly, Miss Matthews really did understand about that. And Dr. Barry had been so nice about it. He had written Sue a note saying that he was very sorry she had had trouble about it, and he had gone to see Miss Matthews, himself, and explain. But that had nothing to do with her work, and it was what Miss Matthews had said about her work that Sue could not forget.

"I wish I might have another night duty pretty soon," she thought wistfully. "I'd like to try again and do a good job of it this time."

She had been alarmed on being told to go to the Women's Surgical Out-Patient for duty. It was an entirely new field of work for her, and she wondered if the Office were testing her by putting her into something different. It did n't occur to her that she might have been sent there because the Women's Surgical was due for a change of nurses, and for no other reason.

The Out-Patient Department was the part of the hospital to which patients came from outside, to receive free treatments. It had a four-story building to itself, and thousands of patients came to the daily clinics. From nine o'clock until noon the broad white corridors swarmed with the poor from the city's slums.

Sue went to it from her ward, at nine, and on that first morning she had walked over with one of the older nurses, who, on learning that Sue was going on duty in the Women's Surgical, remarked: —

"Well, you 'll have plenty to do. But if Nellie likes you, you 'll be all right."

"Who's Nellie?"

"*What!* Don't tell me you never heard of Nellie! Why, she *is* the Women's Surgical. She's been there for thirty years. They say that if you went over there at night you wouldn't find the clinic — because it follows Nellie over to her room."

Sue laughed.

"Yes — but who is Nellie?"

"Nellie's the maid."

"Oh."

Sue thought that she was being teased. On the wards one scarcely saw the maid, to say nothing of worrying about her opinion of the nurses.

The older nurse left her at the entrance to the Out-Patient, and Sue went on alone, feeling very much out of place.

Her first impression of the Out-Patient was of acres of white and gray — white walls, white pillars, white ceilings, and gray concrete floors which had been waxed until they shone. Her progress through it was a progress of odors — acrid and antiseptic from the medical clinics, the smell of ether from the surgical rooms, the warm flat odor of the X-ray department, wet plaster from the Orthopedic, and a pine-woods smell from the skin clinic.

"I could close my eyes and tell where I am by my nose," she thought.

The Women's Surgical was on the second floor, a long row of rooms, all small, and one very large one. As Sue came down the corridor a diminutive figure in the blue and white striped uniform worn by the hospital maids came out of one of the rooms, walking as if she were driving all the world before her. Sue did n't catch a glimpse of her face, but she knew that this must be Nellie, and looked with curiosity at the tiny body and the mop of snow-white hair as presented from the rear.

In the doorway of the large room Sue hesitated, wondering where to go.

A squat, robust nurse with dark stringy hair and an armful of sheets appeared out of nowhere and boomed: —

"Are you Miss Barton?"

"Yes."

"That's fine." She spoke as though Sue had come there expressly for her approval. "I'm the senior in charge," she went on importantly. "We don't have a head nurse. I'm Miss Perkins."

"What shall I do first?" Sue asked, trying not to smile. The senior reminded her of a very puffy walrus, and the loftiness of that "I'm Miss Perkins" amused her.

The senior's round face grew heavy with the consciousness of responsibility.

"I'm very busy," she said in a deep voice. "I won't have time to tell you much. Nellie will show you around."

She moved away, bellowing, "Nellie! Here, Nellie!"

The tiny blue and white figure shot out of a room, ignoring Miss Perkins — who seemed to find it natural.

The white hair turned in Sue's direction, and a pair of eyes which had once been black, but were now oddly dull, met Sue's.

Nellie stood poised as though ready to spring in any direction.

"Good mornin' to ye. Are ye th' new nurse?"

"Yes, I'm Sue Barton. You're Nellie, aren't you? I've heard about you."

"Have ye, now," said Nellie, pleased. "Well, come wid me, an' I'll show ye th' clinic."

They began with the instruments, shining in their cabinets. There were hundreds of them, and Sue was astonished at Nellie's knowledge. She knew the name, uses, and place of every instrument. She knew them intimately, down to the very threads on the screws that held them together. As Sue followed the wiry little figure from room to room she learned all about the sterile supplies, the medicines, the special instruments of each surgeon and why they were used, which doctors liked their gloves put on wet, and which preferred them powdered. Nellie instructed her in the general routine of the clinic and told her how the work was divided.

"An' now," she finished, "it's time th' patients was comin'. I'll have to be puttin' out th' instruments. There ain't much for ye to do yit. I'll call ye." She bustled away.

Sue went out into the corridor to the main staircase and looked over the railing. An orderly was tugging at the doors of the entrance to the building, and as Sue looked they swung open. It was like opening the floodgates to a dam. A black river of humanity poured through, limping, bandaged, haggard, to overflow the first floor and mount in a tide to the second, and the third, and the fourth. With it mounted the babble of languages, the scuffling of feet, and the sour smell of unwashed bodies.

Agitated husbands lost track of their wives and shouted through the corridors; babies cried; young girls, their faces a mask of rouge and powder, tottered past Sue on high heels; young men swaggered; mothers pursued squealing children; old people marooned on settees waited in dumb patience; maids and orderlies ran; nurses appeared and disappeared; house officers dashed.

"It's a madhouse," Sue thought. But she was not long in discovering that under the surface appearance of chaos the Out-Patient Department ran on oiled wheels. Every member of its staff knew precisely what must be done and when and how to do it.

Sue's clinic had five staff surgeons, two house officers, two nurses, one social worker, two maids, and an orderly. Sue fitted into her own especial niche easily, aided by Nellie, who, for the first week, watched over Sue as a mother watches over the first uncertain steps of her baby. There was no chance to make a mistake.

This was a relief, and Sue concentrated all her attention on learning everything the clinic had to offer, which was a great deal. People came with boils, with carbuncles, with broken fingers, with crushed toes, with frozen ears, with splinters in various parts of their anatomy, with tumors and wens and warts, with ingrowing nails, with cuts and burns, with broken arms and bumped heads — and all were taken care of. These were things not likely to be encountered on the wards, but sure to be encountered everywhere outside the hospital in ordinary life. Sue began to feel very capable and efficient.

Nellie was everywhere at once. Sue marveled at the amount of work the little maid accomplished. Her duties, ostensibly, were to keep the rooms clean, to bring up the case histories of the patients, to run errands. Actually, the other maid and the orderly did the cleaning under the lash of Nellie's tongue. They were in constant terror of her. But she took care of all the rest of the clinic while the nurses were busy with the patients. In addition she watched the supplies and told the nurses when anything was needed; she put out the empty medicine bottles for the apothecary's boy; she laid out the instruments and put them away again when the clinic was over.

The nurses were her children, to be loved and scolded and trained.

"Have ye tested th' oxygen tanks yit?" Sue heard her demanding of Miss Perkins one morning.

Miss Perkins's importance collapsed.

"Why, I — why no, Nellie, I was — "

"Thim tanks must be tested ivry mornin'. Ye know it well! Do ye want th' supervisor up here jumpin' on ye wid all four feet? Run away wid ye now, an' do it!"

Often, in the midst of the morning's work, she would pounce upon Sue.

"Come now, darlin'. Impty stomachs make careless hands. I 'll help this lady to dress. Git down to the back room for a bit of crackers an' milk I brought, — before thim others gobbles it all, — else ye'll not be doin' yer work good."

To the house officers Nellie was consistently forbidding. "Don't throw thim scissors on the floor! I seen ye! Look at thim points! Now ye can jist do widout." Or, "Saints presarve us, Dr. Mellow, don't ye know no better than to lave that pail there amongst th' childer? See now, that kid's aten somethin' out of it — hevin knows what. Ye should be ashamed."

"But Nellie — "

"Don't ye Nellie me! Do what I tell ye!"

She treated the staff men with respect, but it was a respect which thinly veiled her conviction that they were naughty but well-meaning little boys who must be humored for the sake of the clinic. Sue came into the big clinic room one day in time to catch Dr. Evans, the senior surgeon, and a man of dignity and importance in the medical world, hiding something behind the radiator. His furtive expression changed to one of blandness as Sue came in. She heard Nellie's voice behind her.

"Shure now, Dr. Evans, sir, I've caught ye. Give me thim rubber gloves."

Dr. Evans laughed.

"All right, Nellie, you tyrant. Take them. They're no good anyway."

"An' why are they no good? Ye cannot tear rubber gloves off yer hands as if they was cast iron. Look at thim!"

She had rescued the gloves from behind the radiator and

spread them out on the desk. The right glove was torn across the palm. Nellie's white hair quivered with indignation and her features drew down into stern lines.

"Ye 'll give th' clinic a bad name, ye will, wid yer haste an' yer tearin's off. What 'll I do wid ye?"

"Give me another pair," Dr. Evans said, grinning.

"Yes, sir," Nellie said involuntarily. And then, "Anoth — Will ye listen to th' man! How many pairs is it this mornin'? Will ye give me thim back whole, at th' end of th' mornin'?"

"Yes — I promise, Nellie."

When Nellie had gone, Dr. Evans turned to Sue. He looked a little foolish.

"Ah — er — nobody minds Nellie, you know, Miss Barton."

Sue laughed.

"I think you all mind her beautifully."

"Hm. Well — perhaps you 're right. But she 's a good soul. The best in the world. She 'd give her life for any one of us."

"I know it." Sue was serious.

She loved Nellie. The thought of the dauntless spirit in that tiny body had impressed her more, even, than she knew. Nellie, like Miss Cameron, was a part of the tremendous, driving force of the hospital. In her way she, too, was a great woman.

Thinking of these things, Sue remembered the day she had arrived at the hospital. It was only eight months ago, but already that Sue Barton seemed an ignorant little girl, plunging into life as though it were a party. For a great hospital was certainly a complete cross section of life, and if she had learned so much in this short time about people, about work, about herself, how much more she would know by the time she graduated. She thought that the hospital was stimulating because it was a hospital. She did n't realize, as yet, that to have a fixed purpose is always exciting; that, at the age when most girls are still uncertain, and wavering this way and that, she knew where she "was going," and was already on her way. She only felt that somehow faith, loyalty, and steadfastness had made little Nellie as fine as Sue, herself, would like to be some day — in a much broader way, of course, she thought with a sudden glow of ambition. And that, too, was something she would not have thought eight months ago.

One noon when Nellie was inspecting the instruments with her usual tender care before putting them away, Sue noticed that Nellie held each one so close to her face that it nearly touched her nose.

"Are you nearsighted, Nellie?" Sue asked. "Ought n't you to have glasses?"

Nellie exploded.

"*Glasses!* Indade not! Me eyes is perfect! I would n't wear thim things for nobody. I bin here thirty years widout thim, an' I 'm th' only wan av th' ould maids that don't wear thim. Even that Maggie down in Orthopedic 's got thim — an' she come here th' same day as me."

All the Out-Patient knew that Maggie and Nellie had n't spoken to each other in years. It seemed that Nellie, in the rashness of youth, had once taken a position outside the hospital for six months, as maid to a rich woman. Many years later Maggie had taunted Nellie about this, claiming that because of it, she, Maggie, had been longer in the hospital than Nellie. The argument had ended in their having to be separated by force.

Sue wisely said no more about glasses, but she watched Nellie.

"Nellie acts about half blind," she said to Miss Perkins. "She bumps into tables and chairs, and if anything has been put away out of its place, she can't find it to save her soul."

"Well, she can still see a speck the size of a pin point on the sterilizer — but all the same there *is* something wrong with her eyes. I don't know what it is. But she gets worse all the time. One day the staff men will notice it — and then there'll be something doing."

Sue made no further comment, and in a day or two ceased to think about Nellie's eyes, for work in the clinic was increasing. The warmer March days brought out hordes of thinly clad patients who had neglected their ailments all winter rather than face the icy winds.

Early one afternoon, when the clinic was over and Miss Perkins had gone for her afternoon off, Sue was putting away towels when she heard an uproar in the big clinic room — an uproar in which Nellie's voice predominated.

Nellie had been engaged in a feud with the man who polished the floors, and, thinking that if a battle were on it would be worth watching, Sue ran up the corridor and paused in the door of the clinic room, entirely unprepared for the sight that met her eyes.

Nellie's tiny figure in its striped blue and white uniform was in the middle of the room, surrounded by white-coated staff men, who were awkwardly patting her on the back. Tears rolled down her cheeks.

"No! No! No! I wun't have a operation! I tell ye, I wun't!"

"What's this?" Sue asked.

Nellie turned and flung herself into Sue's arms.

"Oh, Miss Barton! They say I got to lave th' place! They say I got to have a operation an' be blind!"

"No, no, Nellie!" Dr. Evans said uncomfortably. "We only said you'd have to go to the Eye and Ear Infirmary for a little while. Then your eyes will be better."

"Ye don't know they'll be better. Ye said so yerself! Ye said it was a chance. An' what if they ain't? Then I can't niver come back! Oh, what'll I do?"

Dr. Evans's voice was unusually gruff.

"But they'll be worse if you don't go, Nellie. And if it does n't turn out well we'll take care of you — all of us. You'll never want for anything as long as you live."

Nellie drew herself up. The tears streamed down her face unheeded.

"I don't want to be took care of! I want to stay here! This place is me life. I don't want no other — just to be here, puttin' out th' instruments an' lookin' afther ye all."

She clung to Sue.

"Don't let thim take me, Miss Barton! Plaze, plaze

don't let thim! Me sterilizer will git all green. Thim young maids is no good. Ye have to watch thim. An' who's to make Jack change th' water in his mop pail?"

She hid her distorted face against Sue's breast, with a choking sob.

One by one the staff men, with guilty faces, slipped out of the room, leaving Sue alone with Nellie's agony. Sue understood why they had gone. They wanted her to persuade Nellie to have this thing done. She held the shuddering little figure close, and her eyes, above Nellie's white hair, wandered over the room. This clinic, just a way station to Sue, was an entire world to one person. Nellie had not needed to wander in search of romance, fulfillment. They were here.

Her loyal feet had trudged away the years on that brown floor. They would have gone on trudging, even in total darkness. Her hands, grown old and tired in the service of the hospital, would still have kept the sterilizer clean. Nellie did n't need to see. The clinic was as familiar to her as her own body, as familiar as her treasures, her beautiful instruments, gleaming in their cabinets. And now her own god, Efficiency, had said that she must go.

Nellie had raised her head and was peering, struggling to see through the darkness before her eyes, to catch one glimpse of Sue's young face, and of the room that was her world.

"Niver agin," Nellie whispered, "to hear th' sterilizer bubblin' of a mornin' — "

"Oh, *don't,* Nellie," Sue choked.

There was no answer.

Sue drew back a little and put her hands on Nellie's shoulders, looking into the clouded eyes.

"Nellie," she said, "just what did Dr. Evans say?"

"He said," Nellie said faintly, "that if I hed a operation now mebbe me eyes will be all right an' mebbe they wun't. If th' operation don't work I'll be blind for good afther it."

"And if you don't have it done?"

"Then, he says, I got about a year. Oh, Miss Barton, lemme hev that year!"

"Nellie," Sue said earnestly, "there must be a good chance or Dr. Evans would n't insist. You know we can't get along without you. Would n't it be better to take that chance, for the clinic, than to have only a year left, to see?"

Nellie drew a long shuddering breath.

"But me year! If I don't do nothin' about me eyes, I'll hev that year. An' I know — sump'n tells me — th' operation wun't work." She was sobbing again. "Plaze, Miss Barton, don't let thim take that year frum me."

"But Nellie, if the operation means that you'll have a great many years instead — "

"No! No! I wun't!"

She broke away from Sue's restraining hands, turned sharply, and ran against the door. For an instant she stood motionless, her back to Sue. When she spoke her voice was defiant.

"Annywan can run into a door."

Sue hesitated. Oh, why had those wretched staff men skipped out and left her?

"Nellie," she said at last, slowly, "are you going to fail us, after all these years? Are you going to let the clinic down — and the hospital? Dr. Evans wants you to have this done because he believes it will keep you with us for a good many years, instead of only one. You know that. Please take the chance."

The blue and white uniform turned around. The door had left a red bruise on Nellie's temple. Sue crossed to her, put an arm around her.

"Please, Nellie. We need you."

Nellie's face relaxed a little.

"Do — do ye like Nellie so much, then? They say nobuddy ain't reely necessary."

"You are, Nellie," Sue put in quickly. "Do it for the clinic."

There was a long silence. Over in the corner the little copper sterilizer sent a jet of steam into the sunlight from the window. An unseen fly buzzed heavily.

Nellie's eyes brimmed suddenly, and a hot tear fell on Sue's hand.

"Where 'll I be ter-morrer, this time?" Nellie said at last.

Sue had won.

Dr. Evans was delighted.

"You 've done splendidly, Miss Barton," he said.

"But Dr. Evans — how much chance has she?"

"About fifty-fifty."

"Oh," Sue wailed. "Then if the operation fails, *I'll* have taken her one year away from her."

"No," the surgeon said gravely. "I shall have done that. It was I who insisted on this."

The news of Nellie's tragedy spread over the hospital, and in Brewster Sue was besieged with questions. She had n't realized how generally Nellie was known, and she was touched by the shocked interest of the nurses.

Nellie was to have her operation the following day, and as the time drew near the possibility of its failure haunted Sue until she could n't sleep, and her food tasted like sawdust. Nellie had pleaded so for her one year. And now — what? Had Sue persuaded her into immediate and total darkness, into a life of sitting and groping? Sue pictured it as she lay awake and motionless that night. She saw Nellie, sitting, always sitting — Nellie, who never sat down. She saw the outstretched hands fumbling, reaching, the hesitant feet. She saw the vital alert face assuming the patient expression of the blind. She saw, before her own eyes, the horrible darkness that would never lift again. She, and she alone, had asked Nellie to go into it. How *could* she have done it?

On her way to the Out-Patient in the morning she passed the Orthopedic clinic as usual. Stout, gray-haired Maggie waddled out to meet her.

"Jist a minit, nuss." Maggie hesitated, looked away, looked back, twisted a button on her sleeve. "Ye're — ye're th' nuss frum Women's Surgical, ain't ye?"

178

"Yes." Sue waited.

"Well, I — I jist — was wantin' ter ask ye — ain't they a maid up there by — by name o' Nellie?"

Sue stifled a grin.

"Oh, yes — Nellie — " she said.

Maggie squirmed.

"Well — 't ain't important — I ain't reely interested — but — but, I — er — I was afther hearin' she's in some sort o' trouble — an' — an' — "

"You're a darling, Maggie!" Sue cried.

Maggie's shiny round face flushed crimson.

"Ye — ye got me wrong, nuss. I got no use fer that Nellie. She's a proud divil. But I thought mebbe — "

"Of course, Maggie! I'll come down especially and tell you how she is the minute I hear."

"Thank ye kindly, nuss." Maggie reached out suddenly to clasp Sue's wrist. "Ye wunt be afther tellin' annywan I was wantin' ter know?"

"No, Maggie, I won't tell."

"Thank ye, nuss."

That afternoon Sue and Miss Perkins went over to the Eye and Ear Infirmary to see Nellie. They were told that she was not yet out of ether, and that it would be two weeks before the success or failure of the operation could be ascertained.

And so, for two weeks, Sue went daily to the Infirmary, to sit in a darkened room and look at the bandages that hid Nellie's face, and tell her all the news of the Out-Patient.

She longed to tell her how Maggie waited eagerly, each day, for the latest bulletin from the Infirmary — but she had promised.

Nellie's room was always filled with flowers. She spoke of them with pride.

"Th' red roses is frum th' staff men. They don't fergit ould Nellie. Th' yeller ones is frum Miss Cameron — "

"Miss Cameron!" Sue cried, astonished. "I did n't know you knew Miss Cameron."

"Shure, an' why not? We bin workin' fer th' place for manny a year. It 's often an' often I seen her come bustin' through th' Out-Patient, wid th' nurses flyin' fer their lives before her — an' she stoppin' ter have a word wid me, afore thim all. Niver a cross word has she said to Nellie."

One day Sue noticed a tight little bunch of marigolds on the table beside Nellie's bed.

"Who sent you the marigolds, Nellie?"

Nellie's bandaged head moved.

"I — I ain't — th' nurses said they come from Orthopedic. I dunno who 'd be after sendin' me flowers frum there. They 're nice, ain't they? I can't see thim, but I can smell thim."

Nellie never spoke, now, of coming back to the Out-Patient. The Infirmary nurses told Sue that she had never asked about her operation, and this silence was more dreadful to Sue than any frantic questioning could have been.

The day that Nellie's bandages came off, Sue was unable to get off duty until late. She did her work mechanically, the thought of Nellie always before her.

Dr. Evans left the clinic at half-past eleven.

"I'm going over to the Infirmary," he said. "Call me there if you need me."

Sue swallowed a lump in her throat.

"Yes, sir."

At noon, realizing that she would not get away from the clinic for some time yet, Sue went to the telephone and with nervous fingers lifted the receiver from the hook.

"Eye and Ear Infirmary, please — Women's Surgical calling."

After a few moments the receiver crackled violently.

"*What?*"

"Squee-eee-ee!" the telephone responded.

"Can you tell me the condition of the patient Nellie Dugan?"

"Wawkquaawkqueee."

"Never mind," Sue said wearily, and hung up the receiver.

There was one other thing she could do. She could use the half hour allowed her for lunch to go to the Infirmary.

"I don't want any lunch, anyway," she thought, and could almost hear Nellie's voice saying, "Impty stomachs makes careless hands!" Dear, faithful old Nellie.

When Sue finally reached the Infirmary the door of Nellie's room was closed. There was a murmur of voices inside, and Sue waited, her eyes on her watch, while the minutes ticked away and the precious half hour became fifteen minutes, then ten, then —

"Come in, won't you, Miss Barton?" It was Nellie's

nurse in the doorway. Neither her voice nor her face told Sue anything whatever.

The room was still quite dark, but the shade had been raised enough to permit a little light to enter.

Nellie was sitting up in bed, clinging to Dr. Evans's hand. Two Infirmary doctors and the nurse stood at the other side of the bed. Sue scarcely saw them. Her eyes were on Nellie's face, her funny little face, free of bandages at last. Nellie's voice greeted her.

"Miss Barton, darlin'! I — I can see yer little red head! Me eyes is all right. I'll be comin' back to th' place!"

"Oh, Nellie!" It was all Sue could manage. She wanted to shout, to jump, to gather Nellie's little body up in her arms and hug it. She wanted to say the right things — and all she could manage was, "Oh, Nellie."

Nellie's new eyes rested on Sue fondly. Then she looked up at Dr. Evans.

"Ain't she th' darlin'? Ivry day she come, bringin' me things. An' look at her now! She can't say nothin'!" Nellie laughed, a happy ringing laugh which was as young as Nellie would always be, as long as she had her work, her clinic, and her place in it.

"I — I have to go now, Nellie," Sue stammered. "I'll be back this afternoon."

"Why — ye're cryin', darlin'! Oh, an' did ye love ould Nellie then? 'T is glad I am."

Sue fled.

On her way past Orthopedic she stopped to see Maggie,

whose sharp eyes softened behind their spectacles as she listened to what Sue had to say. "So — she can see better than iver — to stick her nose in other folks' business." Maggie hesitated. "Might be, ye 'd ask her would she let bygones be bygones an' stick it in me room sometime, fer a cup o' tay, whin she 's about agin."

"Why don't you ask her yourself?"

"Mebbe I will, at that." There was a gleam in Maggie's eyes. "Shure, an' it 's a long while since I 've had me a good fight. These young gals ain't got th' spirit."

XIII

DEMONSTRATION BY WILLIE

THE spring and Nellie returned to the hospital together, and Sue presently left the Out-Patient to go back on the wards again — to the medical side this time.

"We go from surgical to medical and back again like a lot of shuttles," she grumbled to Kit.

"Well, what d' you expect, our first year? Next year, when you 're having diet kitchen and Children's Ward, and Eye and Ear, and Psychopathic, you 'll be griping because you never see the wards."

"Maybe," Sue admitted. "But I 'll bet I don't grumble our third year."

"Why not? Is n't it a good year for grumbling?"

"Well, think of it! Operating room, maternity work, Private Pavilion, and — and if we 're good enough we 'll be head nurses."

"You mean you 'll be a head nurse. I have n't a chance."

"I guess I have n't either," Sue said gloomily. Her failure on night duty still rankled. She added after a moment, "It 's people like Willie who get all the honors. I 'll bet she 's a supervisor two minutes after she graduates."

Sue was working with Lois now, and she had to admit that Willie, in spite of her irritating qualities, was a splen-

184

did nurse. She was quick, neat, and gentle, and her patients had the best of everything.

"It's uncanny, the way she wangles special diets for them," Sue told the girls. "And she swipes clean sheets out of the laundry as soon as it comes, and hides them, so that *her* patients have a complete change of bed linen every day, and the rest of us never have enough sheets."

"Well, heaven deliver me from working with anybody like that," Kit said heartily.

Heaven, it appeared, was deaf to any such plea, for two days after this conversation took place Sue looked up from her bed making to see Kit standing in the doorway of the ward.

"Many happy returns of the day," Kit said briskly. "I've come to report for duty. Where's your head nurse?"

"Oh, Kit! How gorgeous!" Sue tucked in her patient and drew Kit out into the entry. "Are you really here for duty, or just relieving?"

"I'm really here," Kit said lightly. She leaned back against the ice-water tank and went on conversationally: "Aside from you and Willie, who else is here? And what's your head nurse like?"

"Well, there's Miss Harrington — she goes to Out-Patient. She's a good egg, I guess, but we don't see much of her. As for Miss Meredith — I don't know. She's a student head nurse, and she means well, but she's one of these little bits of things with violet eyes, who weeps on the house officers because she has such a hard time and such awful nurses. And she runs complaining to the T.S.O.

every time a soup bowl goes down in the laundry or a thermometer gets broken. I don't think she'll last long."

"My, my! How enchanting! I can hardly wait to meet her."

"Well, you'd better meet her, because I've got to get back to work. Come on. I'll do the honors for you."

They found little Miss Meredith wiping off bottles in the medicine closet. This was the duty of the medicine nurse, and Miss Meredith explained nervously: —

"It's almost time for the supervisor, and Miss Wilmont can't seem to get through her work in time to do this." She went on in the same breath. "How do you do, Miss Van Dyke? I hope you are a capable nurse, for this is a very difficult ward."

She introduced Kit to the patients who would be hers, and when she had finished Lois Wilmont came over, to greet Kit with exactly the right amount of cordiality, and to deliver a kindly warning to the effect that the ward was very difficult.

"Nice little place you've got here," Kit remarked later to Sue. "And so cheerful. What do Willie and Miss Meredith do to amuse the patients — help them plan epitaphs for their tombstones?"

Sue laughed.

"Oh, it's not so bad. Miss Meredith doesn't bother you much. If anything goes wrong she just cries. You get used to it. And Willie really is a worker, and perfectly good-natured. She just likes to feel that she's moving mountains unaided."

186

"Better and better and *better,* as the White Queen said. It's so nice to be a part of one big happy family."

But it was not so bad, as Sue had promised. For a time things went well. Toward the middle of the month sixty new probationers arrived, and Sue's class, no longer the babies of the hospital, and very conscious of their gray and white uniforms, adopted a manner of efficiency and experience for the benefit of the newcomers, who stared, round-eyed and impressed.

Connie reported that they had gone down to their first class with Miss Cameron, excited and confident, with uniforms every which way. Kit had seen them coming back, an hour and a half later, white and shaken.

Rumors flew about the hospital. A probationer on Ward 10 was said to have taken off her shoes in the linen closet and gone to sleep on a pile of laundry, explaining, when aroused, that she always took a nap in the afternoon. A tall, thin girl, reported to have been a country school-teacher, had addressed a second-year medical student in an awed voice as "Sir." The nurses were delighted, and made the student's life miserable by bowing and scraping before him. One of the probationers had undertaken to show Miss Cameron a better way to make a bed.

"Do you suppose we were as bad as that?" Sue wondered.

"Probably," Kit returned. "Anyway, there was a girl in our class who got lost in the subway and had to be rescued by a heroic house officer."

"Er — never mind," Sue put in hastily.

Kit's brown eyes twinkled, but she let the matter drop.

The girls were walking over to the ward from breakfast, and for the first time Sue felt that a nurse's life was too confining. Every window she passed offered her little views of the lawns, misty with green, of budding elms against a soft blue sky. The air was fresh and sweet. Spring had come — but the work on the wards must go on as usual.

Miss Meredith met them at the door of the ward. Her hands fluttered uncertainly.

"Miss Van Dyke," she said, breathless, "Dr. Anderson has ordered slush baths for your typhoid!"

"Slush baths!" Kit exclaimed. "But I thought they were n't given any more."

"I know. They are n't. But he's got some idea in his head — he wants to try them on Mrs. Barnes. Do you think you could give one?"

"Of course," Kit said heartily. "Miss Cameron taught us how. She said we'd probably never have to give one, but we must know how, and all that."

"Oh dear — I'm so glad. She's to have it every day at three. I'll arrange your time off so that you'll be here for it. And you're to keep a special chart."

"Yes, Miss Meredith — and if you don't mind, I'll just run over to my room and get my notes, in case I've forgotten anything."

"Very well, Miss Van Dyke."

Slush baths had once been given for stubbornly high temperatures, but had long since been discontinued as too

drastic. They were exactly what the unpleasant name im-
plied — a bath given in water slushy with ice. A large
rubber sheet was placed under the patient and was made
into an improvised tub by means of tightly rolled blankets
laid under the edges. The patient was then rubbed vigorously with the icy water, which never failed to bring
down the temperature. It was a complicated process in all
its details. Miss Cameron had said that even in the old
days slush baths had been given only rarely, and the patients hated them, with good reason.

Mrs. Barnes was a strong and wiry patient, in good condition considering the length of her illness, but her temperature had been abnormally high, even for a typhoid,
and all efforts to reduce it had failed.

"She stands the shock of the ice water very well," Kit
told Sue after the first bath. "But she certainly raised the
roof. I can't say that I blame her. Anyway, her temperature is down quite a bit, and she looks much better, though
she's mad as hops."

"Do you think she'll refuse to have any more?"

"No, I don't. She adores Dr. Anderson, and anybody
could see that he knows what he's doing. She admits that
she feels better afterward."

The news that slush baths were being given on Ward 8
spread over the hospital, for nurses are always interested
in unusual treatments. Even the patients on Ward 8 eagerly watched Kit's head moving above the top of the
screen around Mrs. Barnes's bed, though it is possible that
their chief interest was in listening to Mrs. Barnes's exple-

tives, which developed both in range and in vigor as the baths continued.

On the third day of the baths, in the morning, Miss Meredith came from the telephone to confront Kit with terrified, misty eyes. She was wringing her hands.

"Miss Van Dyke! Something *terrible* has happened! *Miss Cameron* is coming to the ward this afternoon, with a lot of probationers, to see the slush bath given! Oh, what 'll we do?"

The hot water bag Kit had been filling dropped to the floor with a *glug,* and the water poured out over the linoleum unnoticed. Kit's face was as white as her collar.

"*Miss Cameron!*" she said, when she was able to speak. "But I — I — " she stopped. "Do I have to give it?" she asked faintly.

Miss Meredith's eyes filled. She nodded helplessly.

"She's your patient," she said. "You 've been giving them."

"Very well, Miss Meredith," Kit said. She picked up the hot water bag and went into the laboratory in search of Sue.

"What 'll I do?" she asked desperately, when she had explained. "I *can't* give that slush bath in front of Miss Cameron! I can't! I 'd forget everything! And — and she 'll say — I don't do — my work the — the way she taught me, and — "

"Wait!" An alarming thought had occurred to Sue. "You don't suppose Miss Meredith has forgotten about your being on duty for the bath? When are you off duty? You don't think that — that I'd have to — "

"Let's go and look at the time slip," Kit cried, suddenly hopeful.

The time slip offered no escape for Kit. Sue breathed a deep sigh of relief, and was instantly contrite.

"I did n't mean to be so ghoulish," she said. "I honestly don't want you to give it any more than I want myself to — only you 've had more practice at it, and — "

"That's all right, old thing. Don't think I did n't understand. It's every man for himself in a mess like this. We 're only human. Let's see — you go off at three, when I come back. Harrington will be in the Out-Patient probably. There's no hope there. Willie's off now, and will be back in a minute — in time for me to go off. She 'll be here the rest of the day, but — oh, it's no use!"

Kit was nearer to tears than Sue had ever seen her, as they went back to the laboratory.

"Is n't there *any* way you can get out of it?"

Kit shook her head.

"Not a chance. It would only mean that Willie, or even Miss Meredith, would have to give it. Now I 've got my second wind, I would n't wish that job on anybody — not even Willie."

"Ssssh. Here she comes."

Willie, just returned to duty, and very trim in a fresh uniform, came briskly into the laboratory and paused to survey the girls, who were perched, side by side, on the edge of the bathtub.

"Well, well, Van," she remarked. "What's this I hear

about you and Miss Cameron? It's quite an honor."

Kit seemed on the point of bursting, but she only said: —

"Oh, yes. Miss Cameron and I are practically insepar-
able now, though I fear we're about to be all broken up
about each other very soon."

"Don't be absurd. It's a great honor."

Kit burst this time.

"*Honor!* Willie, if I didn't know how refined you are
I'd put that down to bad taste in humor. Honor!"

"Really, Willie," Sue interrupted crossly, "come down
off the heights before there's a dull sickening thud."

Willie ignored her.

"What do you mean, Van?" she insisted.

"I mean," Kit said, "that I don't believe Flossie Nightingale herself would think there was much choice between
giving that slush bath and being shot at dawn."

Willie's chin lifted. She looked down her long nose at
Kit.

"Do you really feel like that? I don't see why."

Kit was ominously patient.

"Well, look — maybe you remember that Miss Cameron
can be quite insistent on your making every move exactly
as she taught it, and in the same order. If I so much as
lay something down on the wrong side of the table I'm
done for. I think I give a pretty good slush bath, and I
give it the way she taught it — very nearly. The essentials are all hers. But having her standing there will rattle
me so that even my now good essentials will go haywire."

Sue, watching, saw the smug mask settling over Willie's face and sighed wearily.

"You ought," Willie was saying, "to get into the habit of doing things exactly right — not almost right. Then, when anything like this comes up, the proper procedure would be second nature to you."

"Oh, go away, Willie," Kit moaned. "I suppose *you* would n't mind giving this slush bath a bit — even without any practice."

"I certainly would n't mind. I 'd be delighted. I 've an excellent memory, and I 'm not ashamed of my work. I 've no reason to be afraid of Miss Cameron." She turned away, leaving the girls speechless.

Kit broke the silence.

"Sue," she said gravely, "I 've just made an important decision. As I recall, at three o'clock you are off duty, and Harrington is in the Out-Patient."

"Why, yes — " Sue said — "but I don't see — "

Kit's serious expression did not change.

"Ever since we 've been in training," she said, "I 've prayed that Willie would be struck by lightning. I 'm altering that a little. From now until three this afternoon I 'm going to pray that *I* get struck by lightning."

Kit's altered prayer, however, remained unanswered. She went off duty pale, but in depressingly good health, and when she was absent from lunch Sue learned that she was shut in her room with vast quantities of literature pertaining to slush baths.

"She's got *everybody's* notes," Hilda Grayson said. "And she's practising — using Grace's teddy bear for a patient."

On the ward Willie went about her work with a manner so pointedly superior that Sue longed to shake her. Willie's nose, Sue thought, was even longer than usual, and her eyes were mere slits of complacency. She was ostentatiously helpful to Miss Meredith, who was running here and there in apprehensive haste, straightening charts, and dusting and redusting Mrs. Barnes's bed, which seemed to fascinate her. Mrs. Barnes was indifferent to the entire matter. If the probationers could be shown how to be as good as Miss Van, they were welcome to come, she said.

Willie put away the laundry in geometric perfection. Willie saw to it that the spreads on the patients' beds were smooth and beautiful to look upon. Willie kept an eye on the ward temperature. Willie put fresh towels on the racks. Willie polished all the bedside tables in the vicinity of Mrs. Barnes.

Sue was left to do the work that made no showing. She rushed in and out with trays and medicines and drinks and hot water bags. She filled ice caps. She rearranged pillows. She did errands. It was when she was coming up the stairs from a trip to the apothecary's that the telephone rang. Sue answered it.

"Ward M. Miss Barton speaking."

A voice said crisply: "Miss Van Dyke is wanted in the Training School Office at once."

Sue glanced at the clock. Five minutes to three.

"Miss Van Dyke is still off duty," she said. "Shall I tell her when she comes back?"

"No," the voice returned. "We will call her at the Nurses' Home." The receiver clicked.

Sue's mind scurried among the events of the past few days. *What* had Kit done now? She could think of nothing. Still . . .

Miss Meredith's distraught voice interrupted her.

"Miss Barton, *where* is Miss Van Dyke? It's almost three! Miss Cameron will be here any minute!"

Sue turned, wide-eyed.

"Oh, Miss Meredith — she's wanted in the T.S.O. They've just sent for her. I don't *know* when she'll be back!"

"I might have known — " Miss Meredith wailed. "Oh, why do these things have to happen. I — oh, dear — you'll have to give the slush bath!"

Sue's heart turned completely over. Then she remembered.

"I'm off duty, Miss Meredith."

"Oh — I'd forgotten. How simply dreadful — I don't know — oh, there's Miss Wilmont! *Miss Wilmont!*"

Willie presented herself, all politeness and eager attention. Miss Meredith looked at her hysterically.

"Miss Wilmont — Miss Van Dyke has been called to the office. You'll have to give the slush bath!"

Willie's clear color faded to ivory and then to a faint green. Her mouth hung partly open. Sue leaned against the telephone and stared at her gravely. Willie made an effort, closed her mouth, and mumbled: —

"Certainly, Miss Meredith. I'd be delighted."

Miss Meredith fled to the ward, calling over her shoulder: —

"Get your equipment, then — and *hurry!*"

Willie's sagging figure straightened. She made one step in the direction of the linen closet when Sue spoke.

"Look, Willie," she said, "don't you want me to run over to your room and get your notes for you? You might like to brush up a little."

The smile on poor Willie's face was ghastly in its stiffness.

"Thanks," she said, in an attempt at brightness. "I won't need it. I know all that perfectly."

When she was gone Sue retreated to the linen closet. She was off duty now, but she could not go. A horrid fascination held her, and from the safe dimness of the linen closet she presently heard the tramping of many feet on the stone stairs. She withdrew behind a row of lockers and a moment later, peering out, saw Willie dart through the door, snatch a towel from the shelf, and dash away again. Mrs. Barnes's bed was next to the door opening into the little examining room, and the examining room opened on the linen closet. Sue crept to the door and listened.

A screen rolled across the floor of the ward. There was a sound of rustling aprons and scuffling feet. There was a silence. Then Miss Cameron's voice, so close that Sue jumped, said kindly: —

"That's very nice, Miss Wilmont." The direction of the voice changed. "Miss Wilmont was one of my best students," it remarked.

"And is Willie purring," Sue thought. "Drat her — she always makes her brags good. That's the worst thing about her."

There was another silence.

Sue considered going off duty. This wasn't going to be so exciting, after all. She changed her mind with startling suddenness, for Miss Cameron's voice thundered: —

"*What are you doing?*"

Willie's reply was breathless with shock.

"Why — I — I thought — "

"Nonsense! You didn't think at all! Repeat that process!"

"B — but — "

"*Do as I say!*"

"Yes, Miss Cameron."

Sue waited with pounding heart. Laughter rose in her throat, but it wasn't amused laughter. It was almost like crying. Poor Willie. Her absurdity, her pompousness, were forgotten. Sue agonized with her, choking back the laughter that was so close to tears.

Miss Cameron's voice came again.

"*Miss Wilmont!*"

Something fell to the floor with a crash, and Mrs. Barnes

197

moaned. Miss Cameron's voice was like the crack of a whip.

"You're very clumsy, Miss Wilmont. Pick that up, and go on!"

Someone whispered, behind Sue: —

"Mercy on us! What's happening? Sounds like a cattle show."

It was Miss Harrington, returned from Out-Patient. Sue explained in a breathless whisper, and the two girls stood close together, listening.

"Am I to bring all these young women here to see an exhibition like this? *Put that down!*"

"Yes, Miss Cameron."

Mrs. Barnes muttered something, and Miss Cameron spoke to her in a voice so gentle, so kind and understanding, that Sue gasped at the contrast, and slipped into the examining room. Miss Harrington crept after her. They could see one side of the screen around the bed. There was a forest of legs below it, and Miss Cameron's cap towered above. Willie's labored breathing was distinctly audible. Mrs. Barnes remarked with sudden clearness: —

"Miss Van don't do it that way. I want Miss Van!"

"Where is Miss Van Dyke?" Miss Cameron snapped, and Miss Meredith's fluttering voice replied: —

"She — she was called to the Office, Miss Cameron."

"Oh. Too bad. Go on, Miss Wilmont! What are you waiting for?"

An apron rustled in the linen closet and Kit appeared

in the doorway of the examining room. She seemed on the point of bursting.

"I — it is n't *Willie?*" she hissed.

Sue nodded. Then, as there was no further comment from behind the screen, she murmured in Kit's ear: —

"What happened? What did you do you ought n't?"

"I did n't — I mean — it was my room. I left a stocking hanging on my mirror — and I forgot to strip the bed. They — "

An outcry came, simultaneously, from Mrs. Barnes, Miss Cameron, and Willie. Miss Cameron's voice followed the outcry.

"Is this the way you remember what I teach you? *Give me that!*"

Kit clung to Sue. Her shoulders shook, but her eyes were wide with horror. Sue began to laugh, and a moment later heard an hysterical gasp from Miss Harrington, who faltered: —

"I — I 'm not really laughing — inside. It 's — more like crying. I — I can't seem to — help it!"

"Neither — can — I!" Kit's whisper was weak. "And I 've got — to — report — for duty — right now!"

Sue controlled herself with an effort and laid her hands on Kit's shoulders.

"Stop it!" she commanded. "You 've got to stop! *Kit!*"

Kit struggled upright.

"I — I 'll be all right now."

A few moments later Sue and Miss Harrington heard her voice speaking to Miss Meredith. Mrs. Barnes heard it, also, and shrieked, "There's Miss Van! I want Miss Van!"

Miss Cameron interrupted her.

"Miss Meredith, send Miss Van Dyke here, please — at once!"

Sue gripped Miss Harrington's hand.

"Oh, my goodness!" she whispered. "Poor Kitty! What'll she do?"

"She'd better give a good slush bath," Miss Harrington said darkly.

Miss Cameron's uniform rustled impatiently behind the screen.

"Come! Come! We've had enough delay! No, Miss Wilmont, you will stay here! *Miss Van Dyke!*"

"Cross your fingers, Harrington," Sue murmured.

There was a silence broken only by the splashing of water and the muttered imprecations of Mrs. Barnes. The silence continued for three minutes — for five. A horrid thought crept into Sue's mind. Perhaps Miss Cameron, wishing to have the slush bath finished on Mrs. Barnes's account, was waiting until it was over to demolish Kit. Sue moaned faintly.

Presently she heard a relieved sigh from Mrs. Barnes, and then the sticky sound of a wet rubber sheet being moved. Rustlings followed.

Miss Cameron spoke at last.

"That was very nicely done, Miss Van Dyke."

Sue and Miss Harrington looked at each other. Such high praise from Miss Cameron was earned only by the utmost perfection. But there was no time for the girls to indulge in mental cheers for Kit. They must n't be found snooping. Sue made a dash for the kitchen, with Miss Harrington close behind. They were not a moment too soon. Their aprons had just fluttered out of sight around the corner when Miss Cameron bounded through the linen closet followed by her flock. The tramp of feet receded down the stairs.

A moment later Willie hurried out of the ward, unaware of the two girls who watched her, round-eyed. At the door of the laboratory she stopped and leaned against the wall, head thrown back, eyes closed. Beads of perspiration stood out on her forehead and two bright spots of color burned in her cheeks. A lump rose in Sue's throat.

It was not until Kit emerged from the ward carrying a tray heavily loaded with equipment that Willie stirred, opened her eyes, and stepped forward, taking the tray from Kit.

"I 'll do that, Van," she said through stiff lips.

"Don't bother, Willie," Kit said gently. "You did all the hard part of the slush bath. You must be dead."

Willie shook her head. "I 'm not a bit tired. It was nothing to do." Her anguished eyes met Kit's and found in them no trace of laughter. Willie's lips trembled.

"That — that was an awfully good slush bath, Van," she said bravely.

Kit swallowed.

"I've had a lot of practice," she said. "I've spent the last three hours learning the whole exact process by heart. If I'd had to do it at a moment's notice as you did I'd probably have been expelled. Here, give me that tray!"

Willie surrendered the tray. There was a moment of awkward silence. Kit glanced once at Willie's face and looked away.

"Van — " Willie faltered.

"Never mind, old thing," Kit said quickly. "It's perfectly all right."

But Willie was thorough as always. "Van," she began again, "I — you — " her voice broke. "You're an awfully fine person!" she said in a rush, and bolted for the linen closet.

Kit set the tray down on the corner of the sink, balancing it carefully. When she faced the girls her lashes were wet.

"If," she said to them slowly, "you ever, either of you, breathe one word of this around the hospital, I'll never speak to you again!"

XIV

THE MIRACLE

WHEN the warm weather began in earnest Sue made a discovery. She found that it was very easy, on her free afternoons, or in the evenings, to get out into the country. During the autumn and winter the city had seemed vast and sprawling. There would have been nothing to do outside it except walk, and walking was one thing that no longer appealed to Sue as recreation. But now, seeing so many of the nurses hurrying away from the hospital on their afternoons off, dressed in old clothes and tennis shoes, she made inquiries. They were going canoeing. The blue distance that Sue could see from the roof of the Nurses' Home was veined with rivers.

All through the spring and early summer, with Kit and Connie, she explored the streams, drifting idly among the lily pads under the hot sun. They went, too, on moonlight nights, when the canoe pushed silently through curling mists, white under the moon, and the smell of damp earth and pine needles was achingly sweet after the stark cleanliness of the hospital. It was good to be away from the bustle and responsibility for a while, to loaf and talk and read.

The hot weather had brought other changes, too. Winter uniforms had been put away, and the nurses appeared in short sleeves and low collars. Classes had ceased with the final examinations in June. Two of the convalescent wards were moved out onto the lawns, in tents, and July found Connie on night duty there. Kit was still on the medical wards, but Sue had been sent to Skin, where she spent an interminable month smearing morose patients with vile-smelling ointments. The work was interesting, but Sue did n't like it as she had liked her other duty. The patients were gloomy and irritable, and the ward, in spite of open windows and electric fans, always seemed stuffy. Sue's best-fitting aprons collected strange spots which would not come out.

On Ward 2 she found herself in a different world. At least two thirds of the patients had had bone deformities from birth. Ward 2 was no dreary hiatus in their lives. It brought them change, companionship — hope. Ever since they could remember they had been cripples. They had been stared at on the street. They had been pitied. Some had been laughed at. But here, on this friendly ward, they were not different from other people around them. So they lost their shyness and admired each other's little accomplishments, laughed at and with the nurses, made old jokes, were encouraged by each other. Pain did not make them irritable. They were accustomed to it. And each one hoped, some day, to leave the hospital greatly improved or quite cured. So they were gay, and patient, submitting to the torture of dragging weights and heavy plaster casts without complaint.

THE MIRACLE

The ward had a short corridor of private rooms and a nursery, with an open ward at either end, one for the men and another for the women. The ward had its own operating room in the basement. Miss Rice, the head nurse, was large and round-shouldered, with an amiable face and a uniform skirt that always sagged in the back. She had been head nurse on Ward 2 for a long time, and ran it smoothly, without effort. The moment Sue came into the ward she knew that she would be happy there.

She was given five patients in the men's ward, but she occasionally helped the nurses who had the private rooms. One of the patients in these rooms was a graduate nurse. Sue read her case history with a mixture of horror and admiration. The nurse, whose name was Miss Phelps, had been on private duty. Her patient, a young girl recovering from a nervous breakdown, had seemed normal for some time and was allowed to go for long walks accompanied by Miss Phelps. One day, walking along a highway near the sanitarium, the girl, without an instant's warning, had flung herself in front of a passing truck. Miss Phelps had sprung after her, hurling her out of danger just in time, but the truck had struck Miss Phelps, breaking her back. She had been on Ward 2 for four months.

"She's a darling," Sue told the girls. "She never makes a fuss, and she's so gentle and sweet. I don't see how she ever had the courage — " Sue paused, and then continued more slowly, "they say the instinct for self-preservation is the strongest instinct we have. If that's really so, I don't see why she did n't jump the other way in spite of herself, do you?"

"I don't know," Connie said. "I suppose training has a lot to do with it. The 'patient first' idea. It has to be sort of second nature, or you 'd just look out for your·self."

The girls were on the roof of Brewster, where the evening air was cool and fresh. Kit was stretched out in a hammock, Connie perched on the parapet where she could look out across the darkening city, and Sue sat cross-legged on the floor. Kit spoke suddenly.

"I don't believe training can give it to you," she said. "I think it 's something in yourself."

"Well, how do you know you have it?" Sue asked.

"You can't know, unless something happens. I think it 's either there or it is n't. If it 's there it will make you a better nurse — it will come out in little things that are n't heroic at all."

"Do you mean," Connie said, "that if it is n't in you, then you 'd never become the really ideal nurse?"

"I don't know — I think so."

"Well," Sue turned her head to let the wind blow against her face, "what is an ideal nurse, anyway? Why should one want to be one?"

Kit grunted. "Search me!"

"Because," Connie said seriously, "what 's the good of half doing a thing — of being mediocre? You might as well have some goal of perfection even if you can't reach it. It 's — it 's more fun, if you like."

"All right," Sue returned. "What's your idea of the perfect nurse, Kit? Let's have a few pearls of wisdom."

Kit turned on her side and stared at her friends musingly.

"Since we're going in for this," she said at last, "I think that the ideal nurse is one who understands what kind of physical comfort will give her patient most peace of mind — little things like color in the room, the furniture arranged so that it's restful to look at — when to talk and when not to — flowers on the tray, and all that."

"But that's purely mechanical nursing," Connie interrupted.

"It isn't unless you do it mechanically. The way I mean, you do it with everything in you, and it has quite a different effect on the patient."

"That's all very well," Connie said. "But it isn't enough. What about the patient's interests and emotions?"

"When you're sick you aren't interested in anything much."

"Don't be an idiot, Kit! Of course you are! And anyway, if you're interested and amused you aren't thinking about your symptoms all the time."

"Well, I don't think people like a nurse meddling with their inner lives. All they want is to be made perfectly comfortable." Kit turned to Sue. "What do you think, Bat?"

Sue ran her fingers through her hair.

"I don't know," she said slowly. "I should say you

were both right and both wrong. Seems to me you've left out the most important thing."

"What's that?" Kit and Connie said with one voice.

"The patient's attitude."

"Attitude?"

"Certainly. When people are sick they need something to steady them — some — some idea. It depends on the person. Maybe it's just being a good sport, or a noble martyr, or — or thinking they'll get well twice as quickly if they put their mind to it."

"But, my lamb," Connie said, "you can't make people think anything you want them to."

"Maybe not," Sue admitted. "But you can help them think the way *they* want to. Nobody likes being frightened, or bored, or terribly nervous. They always try to hang onto something, and if you pay attention and find out what it is you can encourage them along that line."

"But — "

"Now wait, Kit. Lemme finish. If they haven't anything to steady them they're miserable, no matter how good a bath you can give, or how many stories you tell them. If they have something to steady them, *then* the other things just make being sick that much easier. Don't you see?"

"Yes, I see," Kit said. "I hadn't thought of it that way. Maybe you're right. Only I don't think everybody can do it."

"I didn't say they could. You asked me my idea of the perfect nurse, and I'm telling you."

"Oh! All right. Well, let's go to bed. I'm too tired to think, anyway."

They went to bed, but Sue did n't forget the discussion, and a few days later, on the ward, she found a patient on whom none of their theories would work.

The patient was a middle-aged Italian woman with a compound fracture of the hip. After her operation she had been put into one of the private rooms because her continual wails disturbed the other patients.

Sue explained the situation to the girls.

"What can you do?" she asked. "She does n't want anything done for her — it's a struggle to make her bed. She does n't speak any English, so you can't go into her emotions, or interests or ideas. She is n't in any pain now — we had the interpreter over to ask her where it hurt. The interpreter told her please not to yell so, and she said she would if she wanted to. So that's that."

"Does n't sympathy do any good?" Connie asked, still clinging to her theory.

"My dear, one little pat on the hand and she bellows like anything. She adores an audience."

"Well, I don't know then. I guess you can't do much."

The nurses on the ward were equally helpless. All day long and all night, at regular intervals, Mrs. Riccino's piercing voice wailed: —

"Oh, Mamma mia! Mamma mia!"

Neither hot drinks, morphine, nor tender care had any effect.

"Don't that woman never sleep?" little Mrs. Wenesky

asked bitterly. "Maybe yet some of us would like to."

"She'll be quiet in a few days, Sophie," Sue promised, without much conviction. And she added quite untruthfully, "Her operation hurts, you know."

"Ach, so! An' did n't my operation hurt? But did Sophie make like the zoo noises?"

"No, you were splendid, Sophie dear." Sue looked down at the plump, freckled little woman. "You'll be going home soon, Sophie, won't you? You've hardly any limp at all, now."

Sophie's round face grew rounder.

"You betcher, Miss Barton. *Lieber Gott!* Listen at her! What is it that she says yet?"

"Mamma mia!" Mrs. Riccino shrieked.

"It means 'Mother,'" Sue explained. "The interpreter says it's what the Italian peasants call the Virgin Mary. Mrs. Riccino is a Catholic, you know."

"It's help she wants? I wish somebuddy would help her keep quiet a little. Maybe I do something, huh?"

"No, no, Sophie! You keep out of there," Sue said firmly. She knew Sophie's propensity for practical jokes. They delighted the ward, but Mrs. Riccino's room was no place for doubtful experiments.

Sue had relief duty that evening and she wondered if, when the ward were quiet, she might be able to do something with Mrs. Riccino. She could try Connie's sympathetic theory again, at least.

Through the rush of the evening work Sue heard the tireless voice shrieking on. Mrs. Riccino had an almost inexhaustible energy and splendid lungs. The other patients commented on both lungs and energy with great freedom, and there was an atmosphere of irritability throughout the ward.

When everyone was settled for the night Sue ventured into Mrs. Riccino's room. A dim light was burning above the bed, faintly outlining the woman's mountainous bulk and disheveled dark head. Encouraged by Sue's appearance she took a deep breath and produced a shriek of such volume and power that Sue was deafened.

She caught one of the tense hands in both her own and spoke a few soothing words. For an instant she thought that Connie had been right. Mrs. Riccino clutched Sue's hands tightly — gratefully, Sue thought at first. Then the woman's features contorted, and, for the benefit of this new audience, she uttered a series of such blood-curdling yells that Sue would have fled from the room had she been able to do so. But Mrs. Riccino's grip on her hands was vise-like. Speech was useless. No ordinary sound could break through the tumult.

Sue stood there helpless, inwardly calling down maledictions on the head of the innocent Connie. In her efforts to hush Mrs. Riccino she did not see a slight movement by the half-open door, and was not aware that someone else was in the room until Mrs. Riccino broke off a shriek in the middle and stared with glassy eyes at the foot of her bed.

Sue turned, startled, to see rising slowly from the floor in the gloom a white and nunlike figure. The head was swathed in white, in which the face made a dim, pink triangle. The room was too dark to see the figure clearly, but in spite of this Sue had no difficulty in recognizing Sophie Wenesky. She wore a long white gown wrapped tightly around her. Her hands were crossed on her breast and her eyes turned upward in saintly contemplation.

A wave of anger choked Sue. Sophie had been told to keep out of Mrs. Riccino's room. She should have been in bed. In addition she was making a joke of Mrs. Riccino's religion.

"You — " she began furiously, and was interrupted by Mrs. Riccino's voice, reduced to a whisper.

"Madre di Dio! E venga!"

Sue understood that, and for a brief and blinding moment saw in the dim white figure what Mrs. Riccino saw — not fat Sophie Wenesky, but the Divine Mother.

The clasp on Sue's hands relaxed. Slowly and with difficulty the Italian woman crossed herself. Her lips moved, but no sound came from them. Even in that dim light Sue could see the look of simple belief on the swarthy face, and there was a glory in the dark Italian eyes that made Sue catch her breath.

Mrs. Riccino's rosary, with its tiny ebony cross, was under the pillow. Sue drew it out and slipped it into the trembling hands of its owner.

"Ave Maria — "

Sue reached up quickly and turned the light bulb. In the sudden darkness she crept to the foot of the bed, clutched Sophie by the neck, and pushed her through the door, closing it after her.

In Mrs. Riccino's room there was blessed silence.

Sue waited a moment. Then: —

"Sophie! You come into the linen closet and take off that operating-room gown and headpiece!"

"Ach! Sure, Miss Barton," said the unrepentant Sophie. "You ain't mad on me, are you?"

"I certainly am. You might have frightened the poor woman into fits. Don't you ever do a thing like that again!"

The laughter faded from Sophie's eyes, leaving them round and frightened.

"Ach! I were only in fun, Miss Barton. I didn't mean nothing. Please don't tell on me."

When Sophie had gone to bed Sue returned to Mrs. Riccino's room and put on the night light again. The dark face smiled up at her, quiet and relaxed. The woman was still too dazed for speech in any language, but when Sue brought her an eggnog she seemed pleased. She smiled again when Sue turned the pillow and gave her an understanding pat on the shoulder.

"You — good," she managed.

Sue went off duty happy. Her theory had been right — even if it had taken a miracle to prove it.

The ward, next day, was all agog over the change in Mrs. Riccino. The patients concluded, after much discussion, that she had become exhausted by her own uproar. Comments from Sophie were conspicuously absent. The nurses were too busy to wonder long, and accepted the change gratefully, for there was no further trouble with Mrs. Riccino.

She lay placid and happy in her hard cast all through the hot August days, while the sun beat down on the ward roof out of a brassy sky. She wanted Sue, and Sue alone, to take care of her, but aside from that she had no preferences and no complaints.

Sue was growing very tired. The work on Ward 2 was exhausting, for the orderly could not be everywhere at once, and though the nurses were forbidden to lift the patients they frequently did so. The heat was enervating, and Sue was aware of an occasional nagging pain in her side, which had begun the day after she had tried to move one of her patients from his bed to a wheel chair, without help.

She had quite forgotten that she had been almost a year in training until one morning the supervisor called her aside and said: —

"Your vacation will begin on September first, Miss Barton." She smiled at Sue's suddenly brightened face. "I 'm sure you need it. You look tired."

Sue was incoherent with excitement. Three whole weeks at home with Mother and Dad and Ted. Three weeks of breakfast in bed and sitting up as late as she pleased!

Later that day, going over to her room, she found Kit

and Connie equally incoherent. Connie's vacation would begin on the same date, and Kit's a week later.

Sue wired home that she was coming, and from that moment was unable to keep her mind on her work. The few remaining days went by in a confusion of packing and daydreams. And then one noon she came off duty and did n't go back. Connie was leaving at the same time, and Kit saw both girls off. As Sue's train pulled out of the station she saw Kit's face, suddenly woebegone — but after all, Kit would n't be alone long. She 'd be going home herself in a few days.

Sue's thoughts leapt ahead of the train, to the three who were waiting for her.

XV

THE PERFECT NURSE

SUE slept almost continually for three days after she arrived home. The first night she had talked until midnight, telling stories of the hospital, while her father and mother listened, proud and pleased, and fifteen-year-old Ted sat grinning with delight and trying not to look impressed. But after that she found that she was even more tired than she had realized, and wanted nothing in the world except sleep. It was a full week before she began to be herself again.

Then there were dances and teas and dinners. Sue's friends, to her surprise, assured her that she had n't changed a bit. Just the same old Sue, they said. Sue wondered at them, for she was not at all the same girl who had gone away a year ago. She had learned how to work; she had had responsibility; and above all she had learned something about human nature, including herself. No, she was not the same old Sue.

At first her friends had asked her about the hospital, but there was no way that she could make them see it as it really was. Their concept of it was so different from the reality that no explanation would suffice.

"Did n't you hate scrubbing floors? Are the head nurses

awful? Isn't it a relief to have fun again after being shut in for a year? Did you faint at your first operation?"

"I haven't seen an operation yet," Sue had returned shortly.

"Haven't seen an *operation?* What do you do, then?"

It was no use. Sue found it easier not to speak about the hospital, and little by little it faded from her mind until there were days when she didn't think of it at all. There was nothing to remind her of it until one day, in the beginning of her third week at home, she answered the telephone absent-mindedly.

"Ward 2, Miss Barton speaking," she said crisply.

A gasp from the other end of the line drew her attention to what she had said. She laughed and apologized. When she had hung up her mother came to stand in the doorway. There was a startled look on her gentle face. Her blue eyes, always so warm when they rested on Sue, were bewildered now.

"Why, Sue!" she said. "I — you — you sounded so grown-up then, and far away. I hadn't realized — "

Sue sprang to her feet and threw her arms around her mother, her firm young cheek against the soft one that her baby hands had used to pat.

"Mummy, darling! I'm never far away from you. Don't ever think it!"

From that moment, however, the hospital took posses-sion of Sue's mind. She began to wonder what had been happening in her absence; what changes had taken place; when classes would begin; where she would go on duty.

It would be pleasant to slip into uniform — winter uniform now — and hear the swish of her shoes on tile and linoleum. The airy feeling of the corridors came back to her sharply, with the smell of floor wax, soapsuds, and ether.

"I'm actually homesick for the hospital," she thought.

She was quite rested now, though the little nagging pain in her side was not entirely gone, and her mother complained that she was too thin.

"Do you think you ought to go back so soon, darling?" she said the day before Sue's departure. "Are you sure you're well? Why not stay another month?"

Sue's head was buried in her trunk, and she laughed silently at the picture of Miss Matthews's face on receiving a letter from Sue, casually announcing that she would not be returning for a while.

"I'm afraid I must go back, Mummy," she said, emerging from the folds of a dress to smile at her mother. She wondered if it were disloyal of her to want to return — to be so eager to do so? Home would always be the dearest place in the world to her. It was a very special place. But her real life was in the hospital now, and it was time to return to it.

The next afternoon, watching the telegraph poles glide past the train window, she remembered how terrified she had been making this same journey a year ago. It was strange now to think of that apprehension, and when the train steamed into the city and Sue descended into the station, she felt that even *it* belonged to her personally.

In the hospital the first thing was to report to the Training School Office. Everywhere were faces she knew. Even the telephone girls greeted her warmly, and in the office the supervisors were all smiles.

She would have her old room, and in the morning would go on duty in the Emergency Ward.

She was back in her own world once more.

Connie arrived an hour or two later, and burst into Sue's room breathless with excitement.

"I've got the next room but one, to yours," she cried, hugging Sue. "Won't it be fun!"

They talked for hours, both at the same time, until the ten-o'clock bell interrupted them with its ruthless command for silence and lights out.

Sue was pleased at the thought of Emergency Ward duty. Except for the Amphitheatre it was the most exciting place in the hospital. All day and all night the ambulances clanged up to the entrance — from the railroad yards — from the water front — from the slums — bringing victims of accidents, of attempted murder, of attempted suicide, of fights and holdups.

The ward itself was a vast white place, honeycombed with small operating rooms, recovery rooms, and dressing rooms. There was one large ward for overnight patients. Miss Bayer, the head nurse, a slim, dark girl, told Sue that the E. W. either had more patients than it could handle or none at all.

"It never rains but it pours," she said.

The other nurse on duty there was Francesca Manson,

and Sue was relieved to find that she was a good worker. Her manner with the patients was sharp and impatient, but she was never actually unkind, and she did what had to be done quickly and well.

"She'd never sacrifice herself for anybody," Sue told Connie. "I can't think why she wants to be a nurse."

"Why don't you ask her?"

"I believe I will."

A day or two later Sue put this query to Francesca as tactfully as she could.

Francesca hesitated a moment before replying. At last she said: —

"You won't understand it — you're too soft. But I'm going to tell you anyway. I don't like the patients, and I never will. But I do like organizing. I'd like to be the head of a big thing like the American Red Cross, — something that is always expanding, — where I'd deal with things like warehouses, and equipment, and the establishment of nursing centres, and never see a patient."

So Francesca, too, had her dream, though it was incredible to Sue that anyone should dislike the patients.

Sue found them endlessly interesting, from the millionaire's little girl who had been thrown from her pony and broken her leg, to the huge negress whose husband had hit her over the head with a lamp.

Human beings, it seemed, were capable of very strange behavior. There was the young girl who had been brought into the hospital unconscious — the result of a slight difference of opinion with her sister. The sister, in the heat of the argument, had thrown a piano stool at her. The girl had been unconscious for three days.

"Why on earth did n't you bring her in before?" the house officer on duty inquired of the family.

They seemed surprised. They had n't thought of it, they said.

A woman arrived in the ambulance one morning, covered with bruises, and with a broken wrist. A huge, burly man accompanied her. He was very much concerned, and said that he must have been a little drunk or he would n't have beaten her so roughly.

The house officer launched into a severe lecture on the subject of wife beating, only to be interrupted by the woman, who sat up on the stretcher, her eyes blazing.

"You got no call to talk to my man like that! He 's got a right to beat me if he wants! I 'm his wife, ain't I? You leave him be!"

A boy of sixteen with a crooked nose came to the Emergency Ward asking to have his nose broken and re-set so that it would be straight. His girl liked him all but his face, he explained earnestly.

Late one afternoon when the ward lights had turned the white walls to ivory, and Sue and Francesca, having for once no patients, were standing at the desk talking, the ambulance drew up at the door, and the stretcher-bearers brought in a very old and wrinkled man. He was shivering with a violent chill, and had collapsed on the street.

He was carried into one of the little operating rooms

and laid on a heated table. Francesca had vanished. Dr. Reeves, the junior house officer, was on duty.

"It looks like a malaria chill," he said. "Get him comfortable, Miss Barton, and then I'll see him."

Sue took the old man's temperature and pulse, and produced hot water bags and blankets. When she removed the ambulance blanket she noticed that her patient had a wooden leg, the old-fashioned, inexpensive kind, known as a "peg stick."

His eyes were closed and he seemed exhausted. Sue made him as comfortable as she could and was about to call Dr. Reeves when she saw that the wizened eyelids had lifted, and a pair of faded blue eyes were fixed on her face. The operating-room light, on its long arm, glared full upon him.

Sue swung the light away.

"Is that better?" she asked gently.

"Yes, miss, thank ye." His voice was the weak pipe of the very old.

"The poor helpless thing," Sue thought. She'd talk to him a little — make him feel that someone was interested in him.

"Have you had a chill like this before?" she asked.

"Yes, miss. It's the malaria fever. It come, an' my leg went, all at the same time."

"How did you lose your leg?"

"I lost it at Balaklava, miss."

"Balaklava?" Sue said vaguely. The word awoke a thin echo of memory. What had she known about Balaklava? The sixth-grade room at school came back to her with its smell of rubbers, and bananas, and steam heat. She heard again, down the years, a boy's earnest voice reciting: —

> "When can their glory fade? . . .
> Honor the Light Brigade. . . ."

Sue bent over quickly.

"Were — were you in the Crimean War?"

"Yes, miss."

"*Not* in the Light Brigade?"

"I were but twelve, miss — a drummer boy. But I saw the Charge."

"Excuse me just a minute!" Sue rushed out to the desk. "Dr. Reeves!" she gasped. "Do you remember the Charge of the Light Brigade?"

Dr. Reeves looked up from the order book.

"Whoa, there! What's the rush? You're all out of breath. Sure I remember it — who doesn't?" He chanted: —

> "Into the jaws of Death,
> Into the mouth of Hell,
> Rode the six hundred — "

"Listen!" Sue cried. "It's in there — I mean — that old man — he lost his leg at Balaklava! He saw the charge of the Light Brigade!"

"*What!*"

Dr. Reeves sprang to his feet and started for the operat-

223

ing room. Miss Bayer, who had been listening, hurried after him, followed by Sue. Francesca, coming out of one of the recovery rooms, sensed the excitement and quickened her steps.

The three nurses and the young doctor clustered around the tired old figure lying on the table.

Dr. Reeves spoke.

"The nurse tells me you were at the charge of the Light Brigade."

The faded eyes peered up at him.

"That I was. But 't was a long time ago. I was a young feller, then. I 'm — ninety-two now."

"Yes, of course. Could — could you tell us about it?"

But the old eyes had closed. There was a long silence. Then they opened and wandered over the white walls of the operating room.

" 'T war n't like this," he said, and paused. Presently he began again, speaking with an effort.

"Seems like — 't was worse — at night — the heat — like a — hot, wet blanket — stiflin' us — we — we laid on — th' floor — in th' dirt — an' bugs — hundreds of us — an' — an' sometimes they was — a cool breeze — it come — off th' mountains — an' when it come — th' boys all — kinder stirred like — towards it. . . ."

The thin voice died away. The eyes closed again. Neither Dr. Reeves nor the nurses moved. After a moment a wrinkled hand plucked at the blanket. There was a light in the suddenly opened eyes.

"Then *she* come — she — I —"

Sue spoke, a queer tenseness in her voice.

"Who did you say came?" she asked clearly.

The old man moved impatiently.

"W'y — she — our lady — Miss Nightingale — "

"*Oh!*"

Not one of the four knew which of them had uttered that exclamation. The eyes of the three nurses were wide and startled.

"Did you see her, yourself?" Sue asked at last.

"Sartin sure — I seen her. I seen her — on her knees — in th' dirt beside us — dressin' our wounds — hours at — a — a stretch — a lovely young thing — she was — slim — an' gentle. Once — "

He faltered and stopped.

"Yes?" Sue encouraged, and waited patiently.

When the old man spoke again he seemed to have forgotten the thread of his story, but he was still back in those other days, a mangled boy again, lying on the floor of the barracks below the Silver City of the Turks.

"Th' nights," he said. "Them awful nights. She — come then — too — with her lantern — an' water — an' th' rats — run before her — like — like 's if th' floor — was movin' — she — she woulda give — her life — for us — she most did — an' we woulda died for her — God's grace go — with her."

The eyes closed again and remained closed.

Dr. Reeves laid quick fingers on the wrinkled wrist.

"No," he said. "He's asleep. We'd better let him rest."

They withdrew quietly. Dr. Reeves and Miss Bayer went back to the desk. Francesca turned to Sue with shining eyes.

"Think of it — what that one woman did! There was an organizer for you!"

"Yes," Sue returned absently. She had scarcely heard what Francesca was saying. She was thinking of a lovely young thing, "slim she was, an' gentle." She would have given her life . . . she almost did. . . .

There it was again.

The Crimean War had destroyed Florence Nightingale's health. She had never regained it. But there had been another occasion, before that, early in the career of the greatest of all nurses, when she had caught a red-hot falling stovepipe in her arms to prevent its striking a patient. She had been badly burned.

Sue clasped her temples with both hands and stood still in the middle of the corridor.

"Oh, *dear!*" she thought. "I'd never dare! I know it." She shuddered. "To be burned — deliberately — to be terribly hurt — I *could n't!* No matter how much I wanted to, I could n't! I'm a coward. I ought not to be a nurse!"

XVI

THE PROOF OF THE PUDDING

Sue dreamed that she had been run over by a truck. The heavy wheels were crushing her, and there was a stabbing pain. . . .

She awoke, struggling with the bedclothes. A hot darkness smothered her and her head throbbed. She tried to sit up, but the pain tore at her and she sank down gasping. If she could only reach the lamp on her table. . . . She tried again and felt the cool bead on the chain touching the back of her hand — eluding her. She caught it at last and gave a feeble tug.

Yellow light flooded the room. It was her own room. She was n't under a warm, panting truck. She was in bed, in Brewster. She 'd had a nightmare. But the pain still darted and stabbed in her side — in both sides, and the middle. Sue clenched her teeth and stared at the bureau. Her toilet articles lay upon it in orderly indifference.

Connie. Where was Connie?

"I 've been good to them," Sue thought wildly. "Why don't they get up and help me?"

Connie was only two doors away. She must be roused

somehow. Think carefully. Get out of bed. Open the door. Never mind bathrobe. Go to Connie's room.

Sue heard her own voice saying the words over and over. In just a minute she would get up — in just one more minute . . .

The door opened suddenly and a voice said: —

"For heaven's sake, Barton! What's the matter? Are you all right? I heard you talking — "

It was the nurse who had the next room. She bent over the bed and took one look at Sue's flushed cheeks and too bright eyes.

"Where does it hurt you?"

"Everywhere," Sue gasped. "Mostly here." She laid a hand on her abdomen. "Get Connie, will you, please?"

The nurse nodded and was gone. She returned with a sleepy-eyed Connie who became wide-awake the moment she entered the room. She exchanged glances with the other nurse.

"You stay with her," the nurse said. "I'll run and telephone the supervisor."

Sue was dimly aware of a confusion of footsteps and voices, of the night supervisor's face above her, of fingers on her wrist and the cool brittleness of a thermometer in her mouth. Through it all there was Connie's steadying hand on her own hot one. There was a man's voice — Dr. Reeves's? Two men's voices, and the immensity of Dr. Evans, chief of staff, in the doorway — called from his home in the city. The pain went on, stabbing and burning.

Dr. Evans's voice asking questions; Dr. Evans's firm, sure hands touching the pain.

"Get the septic room ready in the Amphitheatre. She's under age? No matter. There isn't time to wait for ether permission from her parents. Wire her father, but get her down at once."

Dr. Evans's big red face and little moustache — his kind blue eyes — his voice again, speaking to Sue, compelling, drawing her mind outward to meet his, away from the pain — his hand on her shoulder.

"You've got an acute appendix, child. We're operating at once. Are you afraid?"

"No. I'm *glad!* Are you going to do it?"

"Do you want me to?"

"Oh, *yes!* Please! I'd rather have you than anyone."

The supervisor smiling — Dr. Evans saying, "When the nurses want you it's a real compliment" — the tiny, hot prick of a needle in her arm — the tramp of feet — arms lifting her — Connie's frightened face — the draughty corridor — the stretcher swaying — this is me, Sue Barton, going to be operated on — the pain growing dull — the slow descent of the elevator — a night nurse in the big brick corridor, staring — the swinging doors of the Amphitheatre bumping — the smell of ether — water running somewhere — the president of the senior class in operating gown and headpiece — "Hello, kid, what d'you mean by it?" — hands fumbling above the dull pain — the cold touch of an iodine swab — *Dr. Barry,* strangely pale.

Sue's head cleared. She was in a white, bare etherizing

room, a little room, with the walls very close above her. Dr. Reeves was wiping the mouthpiece of the gas machine with alcohol, and Dr. Barry was bending over her. His shoulders were very broad and comforting.

"What time is it?" Sue demanded, and remembered that it was the first thing she had ever said to him. He remembered, too, and laughed.

"It's precisely one-thirty to-morrow morning."

His voice was light, casual, an everyday sort of voice, but his lips had no color at all, and the vivid blue of his eyes was almost black. He went on: "How long have you been sick with this without telling anybody?"

"Quite a while, I'm afraid. I'm sorry to have been so stupid, but I thought I'd strained my side on Ward 2. What are you doing down here? Are you assisting Dr. Evans?"

"No." He hesitated. "I came to see you. News travels fast in a hospital. I—I'm frightfully sorry. I—"

"Dr. Reeves—Dr. Evans is almost ready," said a warning voice in the doorway. Sue's heart quickened.

Dr. Reeves sat down on a high stool behind Sue's head, the gas and oxygen mouthpiece in his hand. His smile was very like Ted's.

"*Now!*" Sue thought. She could hear the pounding of her heart, and looked up at Dr. Barry. His eyes held hers steadily.

"Ready?" Dr. Reeves asked.

Sue's voice was firm.

"Quite ready."

The soft rubber of the mouthpiece settled on her face. It was n't at all smothery. She could breathe perfectly. Dr. Reeves laid a folded towel across her eyes, and Sue's hand closed around Dr. Barry's thumb. There was a rushing sound, a cool breeziness against Sue's mouth and nose.

"Just breathe naturally."

Sue breathed, and began to fall through bottomless space. She could n't see clearly because there was a black shadow in the way. Something moved in it — something white. Presently she heard a voice from very far off.

"How is she?"

"She 's coming out, now. I think she 's awake. Awfully good condition, considering."

"Conshiderin' what?" Sue demanded irritably. Something was sticking in her side. She tried to push it away, but her hands were caught and held.

"Here, here! Keep away from that dressing."

Dressing, warm and bulky around her. It hurt.

Sue opened her eyes very wide and the black mist cleared away. Two aprons stood close beside her. Beyond them was a wall, and a door. It must be night, for there was a light on in the room. What had — ? She 'd had an *operation!* And it was all over.

Her eyes followed the line of one of the aprons, past the waistband, up along a starched bib and collar, and came to rest on the face of a senior, a Miss Middleton. Sue knew her slightly.

"Hello," Sue said, thickly.

Miss Middleton was pleased.

"Hello, there," she said. "How do you feel?"

"D-drunk."

"You poor lamb! Any pain?"

Sue moved a leg cautiously.

"A — a little. What — are — you doing here?"

"I'm going to be your night special."

"Oh. Whosh that over there?"

The other apron came forward.

"You're on Ward 3. I'm the ward night nurse."

"Thanksh." Sue closed her eyes.

When she opened them again it was broad daylight.
Ann Middleton was gone and another senior, Vera Durant,
was sitting beside the bed. She rose at once when Sue
stirred.

"How are you, Barton?"

"All right, I guess. Are you my day special?"

"Yes. How's that pain? Want something for it?"

"Please. It's pretty bad."

There was nothing more to do but lie still and recover.
Sue could read and sleep and have visitors. It would be
fun.

But it was not as much fun as Sue had expected. At
the end of two days she came to the conclusion that having
an operation was hard work. There was always something being done to her, no matter how much she wanted
to be quiet. There were baths, alcohol sponges, temperatures, food. The bed must be made, jiggling and shaking. She must drink a great deal of water. She must

have her blood count taken. She must answer questions. She must have her back rubbed.

"And I'd as soon saw a cord of wood as brush my teeth," Sue told Vera Durant.

Vera had smiled and put the toothbrush in Sue's reluctant hand.

Sue was learning about nursing from a new angle. She confided in Kit and Connie when they came to see her.

"Durant does everything beautifully — but that's all she thinks about — I mean, how beautifully she's doing. She rattles around in here, tidying up the room and twitching the bedspread straight when I'm trying to sleep. I'd never realized — "

"Why don't you tell her to get out?" Kit said sharply.

"I hate to. She means so well — and they say nurses are always horrid when they're sick. I'm trying not to be."

"What about your night special?"

"Oh, Middleton's a good egg. She doesn't care whether the spread is straight or not. She can't even keep her own cap straight. And she's got a hand like a ton of lead. Believe me, the right touch *is* awfully important, Kit. You were right. But she's so *glad* to do things for me. She really cares about how I feel. Durant does better work, but she acts as if I were being sick on purpose to annoy her. It's the nurse, not the patient, who needs the right attitude."

"Do you feel awful, Sue?" Connie asked anxiously.

"No, not very. Just terribly tired. I can tell you, when I get back on duty again I'm not going to wear my patients

233

out doing things to them. Honestly — you 've no idea —
I 'm learning an awful lot. Do you remember how Miss
Cameron told us never to bump against a patient's bed?"

"Do I ever!" Kit said. *"My* theory again, angel."

"Well, I used to think she was being overfussy — until
Middleton barged into this bed last night. I suppose she
barely touched it, but it felt like an earthquake. I ached
for an hour afterward. And all that about keeping a
ward quiet — I always thought the wards were as silent
as a graveyard, but this one sounds like the Stock Exchange
on a falling market."

At the end of a week Sue began to have visitors in
earnest. The house officers dropped in at all hours. Her
classmates came to see her in their off-duty time. Supervisors appeared, bringing mail and telegrams, and stayed
to be parental. Dr. Evans made daily visits, and one morning brought old Nellie with him from the Women's
Surgical.

"Me poor little redhead! I 'll be afther comin' to see
ye ivry day, now, darlin'. Th' Office gimme permission."

Then, one noon, Vera Durant rushed into the room.

"Miss Cameron 's at the desk, asking for you. *She 's
coming down here!"*

There was barely time to smooth the top sheet and
straighten the chart before the large whiteness of Miss
Cameron loomed in the doorway. Once again Sue was
stirred by that overwhelming personality, but in a different
way this time, for Sue was a patient now. Miss Cameron's
mere presence in the room brought with it so much vitality

that Sue felt a new tide of life flowing into her weary body.

"Well, Miss Barton! What 's all this? I 'm very sorry. But they tell me you 're getting along nicely."

Conventional words. "But she does n't need to say them," Sue thought. "She just *is,* and you feel better."

She told Miss Waring about it.

"I know," Miss Waring said. "It 's almost a pity she expends herself teaching. But I suppose it goes further in the long run. The school is a monument to her."

Dr. Barry came at least once a day. He drew Sue out, made her talk about herself, her family, her hopes. He had a way of listening which made Sue's every remark seem important. He made her feel attractive and witty. It seemed to Sue, now, that she had known him all her life.

One day, his great length folded in the chair beside her bed, he remarked without looking at her: —

"Well, I shall be through my interneship next month."

Sue looked at him with startled eyes. She had never thought of his leaving the hospital.

"Oh, *no!*" she cried impulsively.

He looked at her then.

"Do you mind?"

"Why, of course I mind!" she said. And then, because his eyes were suddenly warm, she finished, embarrassed, "We — we 've been such friends, you know."

"Oh," he said. "Yes, we have, have n't we?" He rose to his feet and stood looking down at her red curls, tumbled on the pillow, at her startled brown eyes. "Do you know," he said, "that you 're a very lovely person?"

For a moment Sue could find no words. Then she said simply: —

"Thank you."

It was not until he was gone that she realized she had n't asked him what he was going to do when he left the hospital, or where he was going.

Later that day Vera Durant said a little sharply: —

"What's the matter with you, Barton? You're as gloomy as a back yard in the rain."

"Nothing's the matter," Sue returned, irritated. "Except that I feel awfully tired."

Dr. Barry was in a hurry the next time he came, and there was no chance to ask him about his plans for the future. When an opportunity presented itself at last he dismissed the matter casually.

"Oh, I don't know. I have n't decided yet. I 've several openings. How 's the side to-day?"

The side was very much better. It was so much better that Dr. Evans said that the stitches should come out to-morrow, and the next day she could sit up in a chair for half an hour.

Sue felt that sitting up in a chair for half an hour was very little indeed. But when, with the help of Vera and the head nurse, she stood on her feet for the first time since her operation, she realized that half an hour was going to be a long time. Her feet prickled, and her knees almost gave way in the two steps to the chair. Before the half hour was up her smooth white bed was more inviting than she would have dreamed possible.

It was easier the next day, however. Three days later she was actually walking about the ward. She walked bent over, clutching her side, for with every move it felt as if it were coming apart. Dr. Evans watched her with amusement.

"Straighten up, child. Straighten up. It won't hurt you now, if you're careful."

Sue straightened up. It was quite alarming at first, but presently she ceased to think about it. It was fun to wander around the ward, visiting the other patients and talking to the nurses around the desk or in the laboratory. Her special nurses had been taken off as soon as she was able to be up. As she grew stronger she sometimes, in the evening, answered a bell or two for the relief nurse, for the ward was heavy, and the relief nurse was occupied a great deal of the time with a typhoid patient in the room opposite Sue's.

The patient was a young Spanish girl from Peru, newly married to the junior partner of a firm of importers. She had only been in the States a week when she was taken sick.

"She brought it with her, poor thing," the relief nurse told Sue. "Nice way to spend your honeymoon!"

The girl was delirious, and at times very difficult to manage. She was apparently under the impression that the hospital was a jail, and that she was being held there, charged with a crime of which she was innocent. At night, when the moonlight shone through the window of her room, she screamed that the outlines of the panes were bars, holding her in. After two nights of this a special nurse was put on the case.

The special nurse, however, must have food, and when she was away for midnight lunch the night nurse relieved her.

One rainy night, when Sue had tried in vain to sleep, she put on her light, took a book from her bedside table, and began to read. The wind howled around the corners of the ward, and the rain whispered against the window, a sleepy, lulling sound. Sue's eyelids grew heavy. She was almost in a doze, the book still in her hand, when, for no reason at all, she became suddenly wide-awake. There was something strange going on somewhere. Sue listened, but heard nothing. Her uneasiness grew. After a moment she put down her book, slipped out of bed, and pulling on her bathrobe and slippers went to the door of her room. There was no one in sight, but the door of the room opposite was open an inch or two. Without in the least knowing why, Sue crossed the corridor and pushed the door wide open. The light was on, and Sue stood, literally paralyzed, on the threshold.

In one corner of the room, close to the open window, stood the motionless figures of the Spanish girl and the night nurse, in a horrid silence.

The night nurse's face was black, and her eyes bulged. She was pinned against the wall by her patient, whose hands, strong with the madness of delirium, were closed around her throat. That she had been taken by surprise was evident, for she had not cried out.

There was no one but Sue to help her. She 'd be killed. It was then that Sue's eye was caught by something else.

The screen was gone from the window.

The patient had done it. She was trying to escape. And she must not! She must not get out of that window into the rain. She 'd get pneumonia and die!

Sue was so weak still. But she must do something and quickly. Far up the corridor, against the wall by the desk, was the telephone —

The night nurse made a faint, rattling sound.

Sue sprang into the room, snatched a pillow from the bed, and hurled it into the wild, determined face of the patient. The girl relaxed her hold on the night nurse, to fight off this new assailant. The night nurse sank to the floor. Sue could hear her hoarse gasps.

Fingers like iron bands reached for Sue's throat. She fought them off, panting. She was still clinging to the pillow, pressing it against the girl's face with one hand. As long as she could n't see, perhaps . . .

The night nurse was moving.

"Shepherd!" Sue gasped. "Can you hear me?"

"Y-yes."

"The telephone — quickly! I — I can hold her for a little!"

The night nurse crawled toward the door on her hands and knees. She could do nothing, herself, to help Sue.

The pillow slipped to the floor and the frantic dark eyes of the Spanish girl blazed into Sue's. The girl's lips drew

239

back from her teeth. Inch by inch she worked Sue toward the bed. And still she made no sound.

Sue clawed desperately at the lithe body under the short hospital nightgown, as she was forced backward. Now that the night nurse was safe a single thought kept Sue from collapse.

The patient must n't get out of the window . . . pneumonia . . .

Something soft and yielding bulged underfoot. It was the pillow. She stumbled. With an effort she regained her balance. One of the darting, seeking hands was gone. Too late, Sue perceived its whereabouts. It was closing on the leg of the little bedside table. The table swung upward.

There was a blinding crack.

"Must n't — window! Must n't get — out — "

Sue was blind, sick, dizzy. But her hand still clung to something — something that struggled — that must n't — window — pneumonia —

There was a rush of feet — voices. Sue did n't need the thought about the window any more. It could go. Darkness engulfed her.

When she regained consciousness she was in bed. Her head throbbed and her side burned. Something pressed on her forehead. She put up her hand and encountered bandages.

"It 's all right, Miss Barton. Nothing 's broken."

Sue turned her head gingerly, and saw the night supervisor. Behind her was a house officer. Sue stared at them for a moment, bewildered. Then she said slowly: —

"She — she — did n't — get — out the window?"

"No, Miss Barton, she's safe in bed — thanks to your courage."

"Miss — Shepherd?"

"She's in the next room. She's going to be all right."

The house officer bent forward.

"Miss Barton — if you don't feel too badly to talk — I wish you'd tell me how you managed to remain conscious after she hit you with the table."

Sue's mind went back to that dreadful moment.

"It — it was the window."

"The *window?*"

"Never mind," the supervisor interrupted. "I understand what you mean, Miss Barton. Don't bother to explain. You've saved two lives to-night, and that's enough, I think. Try and rest a little now."

When Sue was alone she lay back against her headrest. For a little while the memory of that terrible struggle drove everything else from her mind. Her hands grew clammy with perspiration as she saw again those wild eyes blazing into hers — the wolfish lips drawn back. It was more vivid now than when it had happened.

"But I kept her from getting out the window. She won't have pneumonia. She's going to be all right, the poor thing." On the heels of this thought came another, like a blaze of light. Sue sat bolt upright in bed, regardless of her head or her side.

"Why — I *did* it! I was n't *afraid* — because I did n't

think about me. I only thought she must n't have pneumonia along with typhoid. I — I *am* meant to be a nurse. *And I'm not afraid of night duty any more!"*

The news of the midnight struggle on Ward 3 spread over the hospital like a prairie fire. Kit and Connie were dazed but proud. Sue was besieged with callers, and her room looked like a florist's shop. Miss Matthews made a state visit and said things which left Sue with flushed cheeks and shining eyes.

Most astonishing of all was Dr. Poston. He was the head of the entire hospital, and was so rarely seen by the nurses that his name had taken on the quality of a myth. His tall, soldierly figure almost filled the room. His deep voice overflowed it.

"I want to thank you on behalf of the hospital, Miss — er — Barton. To do such a thing in your weakened condition was most courageous. I trust there will be no ill effects. As soon as you are able you will go home for a long rest. I have written to your parents, myself."

It was Miss Cameron, however, who filled Sue's cup to the brim — with sheer delight.

The austere white figure had surged into the room, looked at Sue for a moment, and said briefly: —

"There's too much fuss about you! You did what you should have done!" She hesitated. "Of course, you were ill. But it's no more than I'd expect of any of my nurses." She glared at Sue. "I'm very proud of you!"

She was gone as suddenly as she had come, leaving Sue deeply touched — and helpless with laughter.

"The sweet old thing! She's afraid my head will be turned."

The day came at last when Sue was to leave the hospital and go home for her long rest. Just as she was saying good-bye to the ward Dr. Barry appeared, for the third time that day.

"I — I've a little news for you," he said, flushing.

"Oh, *what?*"

He leaned back against the wall, trying to keep the pride out of his voice.

"I've just this minute been offered the position of resident surgeon here, for a year. It's a splendid opportunity. I've accepted it."

Sue's eyes lighted.

"Oh, how marvelous! Then you — you'll be here when I come back."

"I most certainly will!"

Kit and Connie had the afternoon off for the express purpose of going to the station with Sue.

"I'm sorry we couldn't bring our brass band," Kit murmured. "But the horns are full of lemon juice."

"We'll sing if you like," Connie offered. She cleared her throat. "Hail the conquering heroine — "

Sue's hand closed over her mouth.

"Come on, you idiots. There's a taxi waiting."

On the station platform Kit and Connie stood side by side looking up at the train window. Sue opened it and leaned out into the smoky air.

"Gee," she said. "I feel as if I were going away forever."

"Not a chance," Kit said. "Your red head will be around under our feet for the next year and a half."

"That will be a feat," Sue retorted, and the girls groaned in unison.

"Help, somebody! She's made a pun!"

The train jerked, and the great arc of the station roof began to move backward.

"Sue!" Connie cried. "When you come back maybe we'll all three have operating room together!"

"Don't you dare set foot in it before I get back," Sue called. "Tell Miss Matthews the white gowns scare you. Tell her anything that'll keep you out of it until I get there!"

The train was gathering speed. The girls' faces were growing smaller — their dear, familiar faces. Sue's throat tightened.

"Good-bye," she faltered.

"We'll be right here in this same place when you come back!" Kit shouted.

The words were almost lost in the slur and click of the wheels, taking her away, taking her home. . . . But they would bring her back again in a little while — in a very little while. She could never stay long away from the hospital. Invisible cords bound her to it, for she was a born nurse. She knew it, now.

About the Author

Helen Dore Boylston was born in Portsmouth, New Hampshire, on April 4, 1895. She left her happy childhood home to attend first Simmons College in Boston, then Massachusetts General Hospital School of Nursing. After graduating in 1915, she enlisted in the Harvard Medical Unit and served as an anesthesiologist with the British Expeditionary Force in France during World War I. During her service, Ms. Boylston achieved the rank of captain. For the two following years, she did relief work for the Red Cross in Italy, Germany, Poland, Russia, and the Balkans. During this time she met Rose Wilder Lane, daughter of Laura Ingalls Wilder, and the two women became close friends.

Ms. Boylston continued her nursing back at Massachusetts General Hospital serving as an instructor of anesthesiology as well as a department director; in New York City she worked as a psychiatric nurse; in a Connecticut hospital she served as a head nurse. In the late 1920s, Ms. Boylston turned her focus to writing.

Ms. Boylston's first book, *Sister: The War Diary of a Nurse* (1927), detailed her wartime experiences. In 1982, long after writing the *Sue Barton* and *Carol Page* series, Ms. Boylston and Ms. Lane published *Travels With Zenobia: Paris to Albania by Model T Ford*, the diary of the two friends' 1926 European excursion in an automobile they named Zenobia. Ms. Boylston also wrote numerous short stories and essays as well as Landmark Book, *Clara Barton: Founder of the American Red Cross*.